Alex caught ...
waited for th...

'So I'm a troglo...

'I didn't say that—your mother did,' Gabi reminded him.

'You started it,' Alex argued as the lift doors swung open. He stood back while she entered, then followed close behind her.

Too close.

'Do you know what the word means? Do you actually know what a troglodyte is?' he asked, his voice still deep and gruff.

Gabi hesitated a moment too long, giving him the chance to answer his own question. 'He's a cave-man, Gabi,' he said softly, standing very close to her and speaking so only she could hear, although the lift was stopping on every floor and more and more people were getting in. 'And do you know what a troglodyte did when he fancied a woman? He flung her over his shoulder and carried her back to his cave, where he threw her down onto a soft pile of animal skins and had his wicked way with her.'

Dear Reader,

Over the last few years I've really enjoyed reading 'relationship' books involving the lives of young, single career women juggling priorities to find enough time for love, friendship, shopping and even basic personal maintenance. Generally, the support network of other single friends keeps them sane, so the idea of helping four friends find love really appealed to me.

Gabi, Kirsten, Alana and Daisy all live in the Near West apartment building, and worked or have worked at the Royal Westside Hospital. Gabi, a doctor, has loved and lost. Kirsten, an occupational therapist, has been held in the grip of unrequited love. Nurse Alana's previous venture into romance has left her preferring the company of her pets; though she strongly believes in love, she theorises that it grows from friendship, not attraction. Daisy is a psychologist, who can tell them why things happen as they do, but can't quite sort out her own problems.

The four friends share each other's tears and laughter, and, often with unexpected consequences, try to help each other along the rocky road to love.

I have had such fun getting to know these women as I wrote these four books, and I hope you enjoy their company as much as I have.

Meredith Webber

Look out for the next three WESTSIDE STORIES:

DEAR DOCTOR (Kirsten's story)
THE DOCTOR'S DESTINY (Alana's story)
DAISY AND THE DOCTOR (Daisy's story)

Coming soon from Medical Romance™

DR GRAHAM'S MARRIAGE

BY
MEREDITH WEBBER

MILLS & BOON®

First published in Great Britain 2002
Harlequin Mills & Boon Limited,
Eton House, 18-24 Paradise Road, Richmond, Surrey TW9 1SR

© Meredith Webber 2002

ISBN 0 263 83418 2

Set in Times Roman 10½ on 12 pt.
03-0103-50123

Printed and bound in Spain
by Litografia Rosés, S.A., Barcelona

CHAPTER ONE

FRIDAY night in A and E was drawing to a close. Not a bad shift for her last night on duty—until next month. Through the glass doors and beyond the ambulance reception area, Gabi could see the streetlights growing dim as the sun began to take over, returning colour to a world bled to blacks and greys by darkness.

Inside the building, the team on the swing shift was working on a patient, but beyond that cubicle all was in readiness for a new influx of patients—the less acutely ill who waited until morning before presenting with their pains and upset stomachs. Full drip bags hung on stands, fresh linen was spread on examination couches and, clustered around the desk, a group of nurses discussed their weekend plans, teasing the intern to bring some friends to a party one of them was holding.

'You're invited too, Gabi,' one of the older nurses said, but Gabi shook her head.

'This weekend I plan to lie in bed, rising occasionally for food or liquid refreshment, flipping channels on cable and generally zoning out. I'm older than you lot and it takes longer for my metabolism to make the change from night to day shifts.'

'Oh, poor old Granny Gabi,' one of the nurses teased, while others, including the intern who'd been pursuing her for weeks, assured her, in the kindest of tones, that thirty was no longer considered old.

'I don't think it ever was.' Gabi wasn't going to let him get away with that one. 'Except to five-year-olds just starting school, when a twenty-four-year old teacher seems ancient.'

'Hey, I'm twenty-four,' the intern protested, and Gabi smiled.

'In fact, thirty-plus is supposed to be the ideal age—you're the in generation these days,' Roz Cooper, the senior nurse and triage expert, reminded her.

'Thanks,' Gabi said. 'I must remember that one day when I'm functioning properly. But this weekend it's "in bed"—that's where this member of the in generation intends to be.'

'Ooh!'

'Who with, Gabi?'

'Anyone we know?'

The wail of an approaching ambulance siren put a stop to the teasing.

'Damn!' Roz said. 'Just when I wanted to get away on time.'

'Did the ambulance call this in?' someone else asked.

But Gabi was already out the door, with two nurses and an orderly wheeling the emergency cart in case the new arrival needed immediate resuscitation.

'No panic!' the ambulance attendant said, slipping out of the driver's seat and passing a sheaf of papers to Gabi. 'He's unconscious but breathing, no blood. The driver of one of those big street-sweeper machines saw him lying in the gutter. Thought it was a bundle of rags at first. We were just returning from that transfer to the chest hospital and pulled up behind the council machine.'

Gabi looked at the pale but beautiful face of the young man on the gurney the second attendant had rolled out of the back of the ambulance.

'Drugs?' she asked, while her heart ached to think of the

loss of innocence or security that must have led this man to this particular moment in time.

'Most likely,' the attendant agreed, but he was edgy, awaiting a signature on the paperwork so he, too, could finish his shift.

'Let's get him inside,' Gabi said, nodding to the other staff, then accompanying the driver into A and E. She led him over to the desk, where she checked the paperwork he'd handed her.

'No ID?'

'None.'

'Well, let's hope he remembers who he is when he wakes up. If not, we'll have to wait for someone to identify him.'

Gabi signed for the unknown patient and, while the clerk took over the paperwork, setting up the admittance procedures and arranging wrist- and leg-bands for him, identifying him by numbers that would follow his progress through the hospital, took a look at him, checking, as always, the ABC of emergency care.

Airway—it was clear but, to be sure, the ambulance attendant had inserted a tube. Breathing—the young man was breathing without assistance, though again, to be sure, he was masked and an extra concentration of oxygen was flowing into his lungs. C stood for circulation which, according to his pulse and blood pressure, was just fine.

So she had to find a reason for him to have passed out.

With help from the orderly, she and the nurse stripped the comatose man, but a superficial examination revealed no obvious injuries, no rigid scars from old needle sites, no recent needle marks. Some bruising on his legs and arms, but more conducive to a fall rather than a beating. She sniffed his breath but found no indication of the fruity breath indicative of ketoacidosis, which would be likely if the coma had been induced by diabetes. She felt his skull—

there was no obvious injury to his head to explain his loss of consciousness.

The nurse eased the unresponsive body into a hospital issue gown.

'I'll take blood for testing, then send him to X-Ray. Could you alert them? We'll let the radiologist on duty decide if he wants scans as well.'

As the nurse bustled off, everyone moving quickly as the end of the shift came closer, Gabi raised a vein in the patient's arm and inserted a needle, intending to take several vials of blood. Test results would come back more quickly if more people were working on the specimens. The process involved leaving the needle in place and attaching new syringes to it, then withdrawing the needle when the final specimen had been taken. Mentally she reviewed the tests she'd request. Drugs, of course, but there were other possibilities. Encephalitis as a result of some infection—and glandular fever came to mind.

She was holding the needle to steady it while she removed the first filled syringe when all hell broke loose. The change from comatose to violent was so sudden, and so totally unexpected, that the nurse who'd just entered the cubicle with the computer-generated labels bearing the patient's numbers was knocked over by his flailing feet, while the man's arm, sweeping upward in an arc to catch Gabi unawares, spun the needle, with the precision of an arrow shot from a sling, straight into the bicep muscle in her upper right arm.

'Don't touch me, don't touch me!' the man was yelling, and his noise, together with the nurse's scream of alarm, brought another nurse, an orderly and two security men all running.

With a calmness she was far from feeling, Gabi removed the needle from her arm, set it on the instrument trolley, squeezed the tiny spot to make it bleed, then dabbed alcohol on the small wound.

Two security men were holding the patient—not roughly, but certainly making sure he could do no further harm.

Ignoring him for the moment, Gabi turned and helped the nurse to her feet, checked she was OK, then suggested she leave.

'Get a drink and something to eat—sit for a while, then go home. It's time you were off duty anyway.'

She bent to collect the papers off the floor, passing them to the newly arrived nurse, telling her to set them aside for the moment. Then, once satisfied order had been more or less restored, she gave her attention to the patient.

'Are you OK?' she asked him. 'You were brought in unconscious so I guess waking up in a strange place freaked you out.'

The young man was sitting on the edge of the gurney, still flanked and held by the security men though he showed no sign of giving more trouble.

'I was unconscious?' he said. 'Damn! I thought I'd thrown that stuff off for ever.'

He went on to explain he was epileptic, though for years medication had controlled his seizures.

Gabi listened, and motioned to the security men to release him, but she was glad the two men remained. Most epilepsy victims she'd treated awoke drowsy and disoriented after a seizure resulting in loss of consciousness. They were confused, certainly, but rarely violent.

'Do you know your name? Address? Do you have someone we can contact? At present you're just a number, so if you could give us some details...'

The young man shrugged.

'Is there any need? I mean, I'm OK now, and I can phone

a friend to come and get me. If I'm not being admitted, do you need to know this stuff?'

'Yes, we do,' Gabi told him. 'It keeps the files tidy and the powers that be happy. An ambulance dropped you off here, we signed for you, and now we can't just let you disappear into the ether. Who knows when someone might turn up and accuse us of losing you?'

She spoke lightly, hoping to dispel the tension she could feel radiating from the as yet unidentified patient. The security men must also be feeling it, for she'd noticed them both tensing—with almost imperceptible movements she hoped only she had seen.

She picked up the file and tried to look as non-threatening as possible—not hard for someone five-six in the medium heels she wore to work.

'Now, if we could start with your name?'

Robin Blair offered this so hesitantly Gabi guessed it was false, while she was almost sure the address he gave, 14 Smith Street, Kirrawee, had been made up on the spot. But he claimed he was just visiting Queensland on business, up from Sydney, and she didn't know the southern city well enough to know if such a suburb existed.

However, it was what she was given, so she filled in the spaces on the file.

'Did you have a wallet with you? Or any valuables on you? Is it likely someone took advantage of your illness to rob you?'

Robin Blair offered her the kind of smile she'd swear had got him out of trouble in the past.

'Nothing on me. All I had were some notes and change. I was out cruising with friends so I left most of my things in the hotel safe. When they went on to a disco I decided to go home. The flashing lights can bring on attacks, so I tend to avoid places like that. If you wouldn't mind passing me my jeans, I'll check if the money's still there.'

'It is—or at least there's a twenty and a fifty and some change in your fob pocket. The ambulancemen found it when searching for some ID and noted it on your file.'

But she wasn't quite ready to pass him his clothes.

'I'd like to do a skull X-ray in case you hit your head when you fell, and possibly a brain scan just to check out what's happening there.' She spoke casually, hoping he'd just agree, knowing they were tests she couldn't, now he was conscious, do without his consent.

He shook his head.

'No way. I'm out of here! Thanks for all you did, but I'm a working man. I've just time to get a cab back to the hotel, shower, change and head for day two of the conference I'm attending.' He smiled almost slyly at Gabi. 'Can't keep a patient against his will, can you?'

'I just need a few more details. Who's your local GP? You should see him—perhaps your medication needs changing.'

'I'll handle that,' Robin assured her, and Gabi went from suspecting lies to outright disbelief. But she couldn't nail his feet to the floor until he told her what she wanted to know, neither could she, as he had so rightly pointed out, keep him against his will.

She handed him his clothes, nodded to the security men to remain in the cubicle and walked out, unconsciously rubbing her arm where the needle had pricked her.

Damn! Her failure to find out more about the mystery patient had left her feeling far wearier than usual after a night on duty. On top of that, there were so many rules and regulations about needle-stick injuries it could be another two hours before she was out of here.

At least she had some of his blood. Or did she? She

looked around, searching for the syringe. She'd dropped the
needle into a bowl but the syringe was gone.

Damn again! Donor blood was always the first thing the
Workplace Health and Safety officer requested. Though
Robin didn't know she had his blood. Was the hospital
legally within its rights keeping it? Or testing it without his
consent?

No way!

Because he'd been unconscious, and not able to give
consent when admitted, she had been legally within her
rights to take it in the first place—to type-match it should
he be bleeding internally and need a transfusion, and to test
for any kind of infection that might have caused him to
lose consciousness.

But now that he was conscious she needed his permission
to test it for hepatitis B and also HIV, however unlikely it
was that he was suffering from either disease. But protocols
were protocols, and the sooner she reported the accidental
needle-stick, the sooner she'd be out of the place.

Which meant seeing the patient again.

He was dressed and obviously about to leave when she
went back into the cubicle.

'I'll only keep you another minute,' she told him. 'When
you were brought in unconscious I took some blood to test
for something that might have caused your loss of consciousness. I don't know if you remember but, coming out
of it, you banged my arm and I jabbed myself with the
needle. You're not in any way responsible, but hospital
regulations say I have to report I was stuck, and the
Workplace Health and Safety officer will also want both
my blood and your blood tested for anything contagious.
Is that OK with you?'

She tried to sound as casual as possible, but knew, from

e moment she mentioned the injury, Robin Blair had ensed up again.

'I don't think so.'

Suspicious as she'd been, she was still staggered by his efusal.

'Do you have a notifiable disease? Is that why you don't want the test done?'

'Of course I haven't!' The look of disgust was well done, ut Gabi had already put him down as a good actor. 'I just on't like people taking my blood. Had too much of it as a kid, with the epilepsy. It's my right to refuse, you know!'

He smiled his charming smile again and walked out, ausing briefly to sign 'Robin Blair' on the discharge form nurse produced.

'If that's his name I'm a Martian,' one of the security en said to her, and Gabi laughed.

'I'm glad I'm not the only one who didn't believe a word e said. And the way he spoke about rights, I wonder if here's a conference for baby lawyers on in town.'

But it left her with a problem, and for a moment she onsidered not reporting the injury, because without donor lood she'd have to be tested regularly until there was no hance of HIV antibodies showing up in her blood.

Muttering grimly to herself, she found the required re-orting forms—one an incident report, the other for her njury—and sat down to complete them. The new shift had rived, but needle-stick injuries were so common no one as commenting on it.

Except for Jenny Thomas, the resident coming on duty.

'Oh, poor you!' she said, after peering over Gabi's shoul-er to see the paperwork. 'This'll keep you from your bed r a couple of hours.'

'Don't I know it!' Gabi groaned. 'Though if he happens

to have been hep. B positive, I guess the precautions a[re] worth it.'

'Did he look like a user, or someone who might be po[s] itive?'

'No, and no, though I'm sure he lied through his tee[th] when he gave his name and address. He positively ooze[d] shiftiness, so he had to be up to something, and didn't wa[nt] to be caught out.'

She finished the paperwork, left the incident report f[or] the clerk to file and took the other paper with her to th[e] staff safety officer.

'I can't believe you didn't get donor blood,' the safe[ty] officer, a woman Gabi had never met before, grumbled, an[d] Gabi, who'd had about as much as she could take, snappe[d]

'Well, I guess I could have got Security to hold hi[m] down while I got some, or I could have scrabbled arour[d] on the floor and found the bit I did get and ignored the fa[ct] it was probably contaminated. Then we could have teste[d] it without his permission and set the hospital up for leg[al] action against it!'

'Now you're being silly!' the woman said, bringir[g] Gabi's personnel file up on her computer. 'Your hep. vaccinations are up to date, but as you don't have don[or] blood—' Gabi considered murder '—we have to give y[ou] a booster. You know the figures?'

'Chances of catching hep. B from a carrier through ne[e] dle-stick injury are something like thirty per cent,' Ga[bi] recited. 'Hence the precautions. But he looked a real[ly] healthy young man. I can't imagine there being any risk[s]

The woman—Gabi couldn't read her name tag as it wa[s] slung low around her neck with the name hidden by th[e] desk—nodded.

'And less than point five per cent with HIV,' she sai[d] tapping information from Gabi's report into the compute[r]

'The jury's still out on whether to treat staff stuck with blood from a positive patient with AZT or not, but staff with needle-stick injury from a known positive patient can opt to have the injection if they wish. However—'

'I haven't any donor blood,' Gabi finished for her. 'I think you've got the message about that across!'

The woman looked up from the screen, the martyred look on her face telling Gabi she was determined to ignore her rudeness.

'You're probably hungry. I have to organise the hep. B shot. Why don't you go down to the canteen and have a coffee and something to eat, then come back up when you're...' she'd probably guessed Gabi might do her physical harm if she'd uttered the words 'feeling better' ...ready.'

Having something to eat was probably a better option than stabbing the safety officer with one of her own pens. It would also pass the time and keep her awake—though she couldn't see why rustling up hepatitis B vaccine should take long.

'I suppose I could,' she said, beyond caring that she sounded bitchy and ungracious.

The woman glanced at her watch.

'It's change of shift, as you know. Could you call back in an hour?'

Gabi held back the sigh which threatened to escape and left the office, heading down to the ground-floor canteen.

She worked along the servery, choosing bacon, scrambled eggs and grilled tomato. The tongs hesitated over the sausages, but she decided enough was enough and settled for a piece of toast instead. Then coffee, because she knew tea wouldn't be strong enough to calm her overstretched nerves right now. She carried the lot to a table in the far corner of the canteen, then realised food was the last thing she wanted.

It was tiredness making her edgy and irritable. Tiredness making the possible consequences of a needle-stick injury bang away in her head.

Contracting hep. B was unlikely because, like all hospital workers, she was regularly vaccinated against it and, unlike some people, her level of immunity was good. But HIV, the insidious virus that lodged in white blood cells, eventually eating up so many of them the body lost its immunity to other diseases, was a different matter.

Gabi stirred sugar into her coffee, then bit into the toast knowing she had to eat something. There was almost more chance of winning the lotto than contracting HIV through a needle-stick injury, so her concern levels weren't high, but the worry with HIV was not knowing.

She prodded the toast into the scrambled eggs, picking up a little bit and nibbling it experimentally. Without donor blood—she rolled her eyes as she thought of the safety officer—to rule out HIV, she'd have to be tested now, then in three months and again in six months. Six months before she'd be cleared of a possible life sentence…

Possible death sentence…

She blinked as if a strong light had been shone on her face, while deep within her body she felt a stirring of an emotion she could only describe as revolt. Then she took another sip of coffee and smiled to herself.

'Damn it all, Gabi Graham—if this isn't exactly what you needed. Something to shock you back to life.'

She glanced around, hoping there was no one close enough to hear her talking to herself, but continued smiling as she fished in one jacket pocket for a pen and in the other for the tiny notebook she always carried with her.

So she had six months before she'd know—six months

n which to grab hold of life and shake all the good out of
t. She'd make a list of all the things she'd always wanted
o do, and work her way through them.

'Go blonde,' she wrote, and underlined it. Would it be
oo late to get an appointment for today? She could always
sleep in the chair.

'No more diets.' They didn't work anyway. She'd accept
she was a natural endomorph, with padded curves instead
of jutting bones.

'New clothes'—boy, wouldn't Kirsten love that one? Her
neighbour was forever trying to talk her into shopping
sprees, but since Alex's departure—or probably, if she was
honest, earlier than that—she'd lost all interest in how she
dressed. She liked to be neat and tidy, but beyond that...

'Take up belly-dancing'—given number two on the list,
she'd have the figure for it. Though maybe not belly-
dancing. Maybe South American dancing—she'd read
about clubs...

'Get over the plane thing.'

If she could get over her fear of heights, and its attendant
fear of flying, she could go on exotic holidays—maybe
Europe, maybe visit Alex in Scotland. Maybe talk to Alex
about what had gone wrong in their marriage. Maybe—

Forget Alex, she told herself sternly. You're doing this
for you.

But getting over the plane hang-up was an excellent idea.
Something really positive she could do for herself—for her
confidence, her self-esteem.

She chewed the end of the pen as she thought about it,
not sure if it was actually possible to be free of a phobia
like this one. Unless she used shock tactics. Like what,
namebrain? a head-voice jeered, then with light bulb bril-
liance the solution flashed upon her.

She could do the basic rescue training course and join

the list of A and E doctors rostered to work on the rescue helicopter. Once she'd been over a cliff on a rope, and dropped out of a helicopter, the phobia might be dead.

Or she might be dead—killed by sheer terror and the embarrassment of everyone else on the course witnessing her cowardice.

But if she survived, she'd either be over it or she'd know for certain it was never going to go away.

Ignoring a quiver of fear already rattling her nerves and making her palms sweat, she steeled herself. She'd check the noticeboard in A and E before she left and put her name down for the next course.

Back to the list.

She thought of some incredibly boring evenings she'd endured at parties she hadn't wanted to attend, and with great deliberation considered the next item, finally writing 'Never waste your free time doing things you don't particularly want to do, or with people you don't like.'

This was a hard one. It would mean saying no to well meaning friends who invited her to dinner and set her up with 'dates', and saying no when Kirsten or Alana insisted she go clubbing with them.

Sometimes going clubbing was OK.

Sometimes she felt like it.

But other evenings she'd rather have her toenails pulled...

And, though she'd enjoyed being married—lie, she'd loved being married—and sometimes ached for what she'd lost, none of the men she'd met since Alex had left had made much of an impression on her. They certainly hadn't come close to producing that tinglingly alive feeling which being near Alex had always generated.

She enjoyed her friends' company, so an occasional night

with them was OK, but no giving in when she didn't feel like it—not any more!

With her out-of-work life covered, she considered her career—where she was now and where, before so many other things had happened to deflect her off track, she had once wanted to be by the time she turned thirty.

She'd wanted to be running the A and E department at a children's hospital. That was where she'd wanted to be.

She might have missed the thirty mark but it wasn't too late for change.

With a determination she hadn't felt for years, and a sudden uplifting of excitement in her heart, she wrote, 'Get some more general paediatrics experience.' In fact, when she went back up to the safety officer, she'd see someone in the human resources department and see if there was any possibility of a shift to the kids' ward on a short rotation, sooner rather than later. The extra experience with kids would help when a job came up at the new children's hospital.

Though, if she was focussing more on kids, was it worth doing the rescue training?

Wimp!

She underlined the training programme, then reread the list and grinned to herself. It mightn't look life-altering, but it represented such huge changes she felt as much apprehension as excitement.

And she'd certainly stopped worrying over HIV infection!

She doodled a border around the list, then, because it was a dream she'd held for a long, long time, she added one more item and doodled another border around it.

'Dance all night in a red dress, then drive to the beach to sit on the sand and watch the sun come up over the ocean.'

It seemed so feeble after the enormous hurdle of gettin
over her fear of heights and her new commitment to he
career, she almost crossed it off, then, mentally chidin
herself for backing out before she'd even begun these li
changes, she added another border of squiggles to empha
sise it.

The massive hep. B booster dampened her enthusiasi
slightly, then realising it was Saturday and no one wa
working in Human Resources put a further hold on he
plans—though she did pick up a slim paper that detaile
current and upcoming hospital vacancies and appointment
Back down in A and E, she wrote her name on the list o
staff willing to do the basic training course to qualify the
for working on the rescue helicopter. Then saw the date.
was next weekend, and once again her palms sweated an
her stomach twisted anxiously.

It's a whole week away, she told her body as sh
marched out of the hospital. And with so much to fit int
the week she'd have no time to think about flinging herse
off the top of a cliff with her life depending on a bit o
rope and her own ability to not panic.

Aaargh!

Think hair instead. She'd sleep, then phone some hai
dressing establishments. If she couldn't get in today, ther
was always tomorrow.

Fearful her determination to change was already weak
ening, she hesitated outside the hospital entrance. The wal
from here to her flat in the Near West apartment buildin
took ten minutes. To get there she turned right, crossed th
main road at the corner, then left into Market Street an
home.

Not good enough! she told herself, and deliberatel
turned left, then left again, circumnavigating the hospital t
come at Market Street from a different angle, walking alon

streets she'd never walked before, looking at houses and apartment blocks she'd possibly seen but never really noticed. The jacarandas were blooming, their purple blossoms spreading an exotic scented carpet beneath her feet. The sun warmed her back and the warmth fed into her blood, renewing her enthusiasm for change so vibrantly she tacked the stairs rather than take the lift to her fourth-floor flat.

'Not such a good idea,' she puffed as she leaned against the fire-escape door on her floor, hoping body weight alone would force it open. It did, but not by much, so she slid through the opening and promptly tripped over something left lying in the passage.

Or someone!

The obstacle moved, sorting itself into a person—male, five-eleven, with red-brown hair and dark brown eyes, and lips that could draw a smile from a statue.

Not that she noticed these features immediately. She just knew them—knew who it was...

'Alex?'

Whether it was climbing the stairs or seeing her ex-husband so unexpectedly she wasn't sure, but the word came out as a quavery and very doubtful squeak, while her legs felt as if they'd lost their stuffing.

She remembered the new Gabi—never spend time with people you don't want to see—and pulled herself together.

'What on earth are you doing here?'

He was running his fingers through his hair, scratching at his scalp, trying to wake up—always a difficult task for Alex.

'Mum. You know she's sick. Didn't sleep on the plane, so when I got here and you weren't home I knew you must be on night duty and you'd be back soon. Had a bit of a kip while I waited.'

He glanced at his watch, then added, 'More than a bit.
You're very late.'

Gabi ignored the unspoken criticism, too incensed by his
earlier assumption.

'You *knew* I must be on night duty?' she repeated. 'At
dawn on a Saturday morning that's the only place I could
possibly be? You didn't think for a minute I might be abseiling down a cliff, or dancing all night with a stranger in
a red dress then watching the sun come up over the ocean?'

Alex looked confused, which, she realised, was hardly
surprising, given how predictable his ex-wife had always
been.

'Never in a million years the abseiling—but a stranger
in a red dress?'

There was so much disbelief in his voice that Gabi lost
it completely.

'Me in a red dress, you idiot. Not the stranger. And what
are you doing here anyway, apart from blocking the fire
exit? Because good old Gabi will put you up! I bet that's
why. Well, let me tell you, buster, good old Gabi no longer
exists. I might look the same, but not for long. Good old
Gabi's gone, and not before time. Miserable creature that
she was—'

'The flat's in my name.'

Alex was standing up now, and it was more that than the
reminder which stopped Gabi's flow of words.

Alex sitting on the floor, still half-asleep, was one thing.
Alex standing, right there in front of her, unconsciously
shedding pheromones the way other people shed skin cells
was a whole other animal.

'I suppose you don't want to stay at your mother's place
with Fred,' she grumbled. 'Honestly, Alex, it's time you
got over that. It would do your mother more good than all

he treatment she's on if you accepted the fact she's re-
married.'

Then she remembered what had happened when Alex
and she had split up and how, because he'd been due to go
overseas four weeks later, he *had* gone to live, temporarily,
with his mother—and Fred.

And Fred's daughter, the beautiful Diane, newly returned
from a modelling assignment in Japan!

Gabi pulled the key out of her handbag and unlocked
her door. Maybe she should let him stay here. And because
Diane Kennedy was a subject never broached between
them, and her new-found confidence was wavering slightly,
she hurried into more conversation.

'I've seen your mother every day—she's very positive.
And having you come home to visit—I assume that's all it
is, a visit?—well, that will cheer her up no end.'

She dumped her handbag on a lounge chair, so aware of
Alex's presence in the flat that her back prickled with pins
and needles. But she had no intention of giving in to pins
and needles or any other physical discomfort being near
Alex might cause. The new Gabi was strong, invincible—
and the ultimate in cool!

'You'll want to see her straight away, so why don't you
have a shower and go on over? I'm going...'

She was far too wired to sleep, so she stopped the words
'to bed' before they had a chance to escape, switching to
'out' just in time to make it sound believable.

Hopefully!

'You're going out when you've just come off duty?'

It must have sounded believable for Alex to be questioning it so disbelievingly!

Cool! she reminded herself. She turned and raised an
eyebrow, an accomplishment that had taken long years of

practice to perfect. Now she used it to remind him that what she did was none of his business.

'I'll have a shower,' he said, proving the eyebrow had retained its potent power, while something that looked almost like uncertainty in his eyes gave Gabi a tingling spurt of pleasure.

Yes! As he turned away, lugging his loaded backpack into the spare bedroom, she pumped the air triumphantly as the affirmation sounded in her head. OK, so it was only a small triumph, but it was a start. If she could surprise Alex at such an early stage of her transformation, then maybe she could succeed.

And by concentrating on the new Gabi she could—perhaps—pretend he wasn't here, wasn't back in the flat they'd shared, albeit in a different bed. Though he'd be with his mother most of the time, she reminded herself when a quiver of what could only be alarm ran through her body.

And when he wasn't visiting at the hospital he'd be catching up with friends.

He'd only use the flat to sleep and change his clothes.

But no assurances could mask the new tension inside her. It was the sound of the shower starting in the bathroom at the exact moment she mentally considered the clothes-changing thing that threw up an image of Alex naked.

In her flat!

Their flat, as it had been.

She squeezed her eyes shut, hoping lack of light might blot out the picture in her mind, then, as something—possibly resolve—crumpled inside her, she straightened, shoring up her weakened defences with reminders of all the reasons she and Alex had split up.

Not least of which had been Diane Kennedy.

No, that was unfair. Diane Kennedy hadn't come into the picture until after they'd split up. And just how far in she'd come, Gabi had never been sure. But seeing Alex out with Diane had been the final nail in the coffin of their marriage as far as Gabi had been concerned. Proof positive that things would never work between them again.

If only she could get her body to accept it, she thought when she glimpsed Alex, his lower abdomen modestly swathed in a towel, crossing the passage from the bathroom to the second bedroom.

A phone book, that was what she needed. Thick yellow pages. Not to rip apart in frustration or hurl at the head of her visitor, but for a hair appointment.

A hairdresser in the trendy El Centro shopping mall had a cancellation at midday. Gabi took it, then headed for the kitchen to find a pack of garbage bags. If she was going to do this, she had to do it properly, and keeping blah clothes that belonged to the old Gabi just wasn't on. She'd pack them into garbage bags and drop them in a charity bin on her way to the hairdresser.

The little boutiques in El Centro would have just the style of clothes the new Gabi needed!

'I'm off. I don't know when I'll be back.' Alex's casual announcement reminded her of her uninvited guest.

'Wait. I'll give you a key. I've no idea when I'll be back either.'

Ha! Second look of surprise on Alex's face. The old Gabi would have waited in for him, made sure she was here, and probably had a meal cooked as well. Talk about a doormat!

Though it hadn't always been that way, she admitted sadly as the door closed behind the man her heart still hungered for. The doormat thing had only begun after she'd lost the baby, and the gap that had started opening up between them even before she'd become pregnant had widened so far she hadn't been able to find a way back to where they'd once been.

And she hadn't been sure that Alex had wanted to find one.

The domesticity route had been suggested by the counsellor she'd seen, but it had angered Alex more than it had appeased him, and in the end the tension and unresolved conflict between them had been so bad it had been a relief to see him go.

Water under the bridge! That was then and this was now! Duh!

She banged her forehead with the palm of her hand. Surely the new Gabi should have said no to Alex's invasion of her flat. After all, the man had friends!

Though having him here would steel her to follow this new path she'd chosen, and—she grinned to herself—seeing his reaction to it all would certainly be entertaining.

She continued to shore up her confidence as she hauled sensible clothes out of her wardrobe and rammed them into garbage bags, continued to remind herself of the new Gabi as she emptied drawers full of sensible undies into another bag for disposal.

Then she came across the dress.

The Dress!

It was red and slinky and she held it against her cheek to feel the cool silkiness. It was a dress like nothing she'd ever worn, bought when she had been less than three months pregnant but already feeling bloated, constantly sick and thoroughly uncomfortable. And although Alex had been insisting they go to Scotland, as planned, she'd still been hoping he'd change his mind.

In her wonderful dream they would stay in Queensland, and by the time the hospital ball came around, she'd figured, when the dress had tempted her from a shop window, the baby she was carrying would be three months old, and she'd leave him—or her—with Alex's mother and they'd go to the ball, dance all night, then drive to the beach to sit on the sand and watch the sun come up over the ocean.

So she'd bought the dress. No matter that Alex hated dancing and that the dream had been as unrealistic—given the state of her marriage and the tickets to Scotland—as the rest of her dreams at that time.

Then she'd lost the baby the next day. But the silly idea must have been hiding in the murky gloom of her subconscious, emerging from the dark depths when she'd written the same thing on her list this morning. 'As if!' she muttered to herself, shoving the red dress into the bag with the undies. She certainly wasn't charitable enough to give it to some other woman to wear for *her* dream.

CHAPTER TWO

THE plastic bag hovered over the dumpster in the maintenance area behind the building, then Gabi withdrew it, pulled out the red dress, slung it over her shoulder and tossed the rest in. The other garbage bags were by the door leading to the steps down to the basement. She picked them up, depressed by the fact that her entire wardrobe of clothes fitted into two garbage bags.

Then she felt the slither of silk against her shoulder and remembered the dress. It was like a red flag of courage, reminding her of her commitment—awaiting the night when she'd wear it to fulfil the final item on the list.

She was so focussed on the future she failed to see the figure, laden with groceries, crossing from a parked car to the lift.

'Are you sleep-walking or what?' Kirsten demanded, and Gabi, blinking to adjust her eyes from the light in the stairwell to the gloom of the basement, chuckled.

'Probably!' she said. 'I'm sure if I was fully conscious I wouldn't be doing this.'

Kirsten's slumberous green eyes took in the garbage bags, and widened in surprise.

'Doing what? You're not moving out?' she wailed. 'Who will I have to talk to if you go? When did you decide? Does Alana know? Oh, Gabi, don't go!'

The plaintive plea lost oomph, and even in the semi-darkness Gabi could see the speculative gleam in Kirsten's eyes.

'Before you get totally carried away, imagining your perfect man shifting into my flat, I'm not going anywhere. I'm just taking all my clothes to the charity bins down the road.'

'You're joining a nudist colony? Or is it a new quirky thing in A and E—just white coats and nothing underneath? Are patient numbers dropping so that you have to try something different? Boy, what would I give to see Eric Cooper's coat flap open!'

'The mind boggles!' Gabi giggled at the picture. 'Can you imagine?'

'So what's it all about? You've won a complete wardrobe from one of the department stores! Oh, great. Let me dump these groceries and I'll come with you. Help you choose. Then we'll ring Alana, and she can find out who else is free, and we'll go out clubbing tonight so you can show them off.'

'No!' Gabi said, remembering her list.

'No, I can't come with you or, no, you won't go out? If it's going out, you always say no at first, then you give in—'

'Only because you and Alana keep on and on at me. This no is a no that I mean—not tonight, Kirsten, because I won't have time to sleep all day.'

'You're going to shop all day?' Kirsten said with such total disbelief Gabi felt her eyes rolling around in her head. She couldn't have avoided seeing Kirsten, but she should have kept her mouth shut about the shopping.

'No!' Gabi said again. 'First I'm going to the hairdresser.'

'You're going to the hairdresser?'

'Is there an echo down here or are you being more than usually dense?' Gabi demanded. She dropped the bags to the ground but resisted the urge to shake her friend. After all, if anyone knew about clothes and style it was Kirsten, and her help and advice on the shopping expedition would be invaluable. 'I'm popping these bags in the bins, going to the hairdresser, then shopping for clothes. Now, do you want to meet me for the shopping part or not?'

'Where?' Suspicion clung to the word, Kirsten no doubt imagining Gabi's usual shopping outings to outlet shops and dreary department stores.

'El Centro.'

'El Centro? You're going shopping in El Centro?'

'It's the echo thing again!' Gabi muttered, then realised she was fast running out of time. 'Look, if you want to come shopping with me, meet me at Luca's Salon at two.'

She walked away with another echo, Kirsten's disbelieving 'Luca's Salon?' ringing in her ears.

Luca himself insisted on overseeing the transformation of Gabi's hair from an indeterminate colour and styleless cut to a shining bob of blonde and hazelnut streaks. She'd been uncertain about the streaks, assuming, given her luck, she'd end up looking like a tiger or, worse, a variegated rug, but when he'd announced she would also be getting a complete make-over, fears about striped hair vanished.

'I'm a minimal make-up kind of person,' she protested, but Luca waved her objections away.

'Minimal is good, but you have to get it right,' he told her, summoning his make-up artist, then poking and prodding at Gabi's skin and facial structure.

'Leave it to Anna!' he finally decreed, and the woman went to work with lotions and potions, then a dash of this and a brush of that and a whisk of something else, bringing out cheekbones Gabi hadn't known existed, and emphasising eyes which had been useful enough in the past to see out of, but were now things of beauty.

Transformation complete, Gabi stared at her image in the mirror, wondering if the inner woman would ever be able to match up to the gleaming confident-looking outer one.

But best of all was Kirsten's double-take when they met in the doorway of the salon—Kirsten stepping aside to let the stranger past, then realising who it was.

'My God! You're beautiful!'

'It's the make-up,' Gabi assured her. 'Underneath that it's just the same old nondescript me.'

'Nonsense! You were never nondescript. In fact, you were very attractive in an understated way—you just kept understating it and understating it until you practically disappeared. All that ex-husband's fault, no doubt.'

This was the moment to tell Kirsten about the ex-husband's return, but as it was only temporary, and Kirsten had never known Alex—and Kirsten was very attractive—Gabi chickened out, suggesting instead they eat before hitting the shops.

Maybe food would shift thoughts of Alex—and Alex's reaction to the new Gabi—out of her head. After all, she was doing this for herself, not for Alex or any man!

Familiar with the shopping centre, Kirsten guided her to 'the best' coffee-shop, then proceeded to outline her plans for the afternoon's sortie.

'We'll start at Starkers, because there's no point in trying on fabulous clothes if you're in your usual sensible underwear. Then move on to Star Signs for casual gear you can wear to work or at weekends around the house, and leave the glamour stuff for last.'

She studied her friend.

'I don't suppose you'd like to buy this gorgeous sexy black-beaded evening gown I saw in Stardust last weekend?'

'Fit both of us, would it?' Gabi teased, then, puzzled by more repetition, asked, 'Do all the shops have "Star" in them?'

'Only the women's clothes shops.' Kirsten grinned at

her. 'The men's use "Stud". Come on, you've had your caffeine fix—let's go.'

And go Gabi did. Determined that if she was doing this at all, she'd do it properly, she dug into the savings she'd been accumulating so diligently over the years, splashing out on matching bra and panty sets—patterned, lacy, stitched with bright flowers—silky camisoles and slinky half-slips that hugged her hips and thighs.

'Nobody'd ever have guessed you had a figure under your daggy old skirts and blouses,' Kirsten remarked, dragging Gabi, new underwear hidden beneath her old work clothes, to the next stage of the expedition.

'They were never daggy,' Gabi protested. 'Just serviceable.'

Had they been daggy? Had Alex thought so? Damn the man—why come back and mess with her head right now, just when she was going for change and confidence.

'Daggy!' Kirsten, not privy to the mental conversation, repeated firmly. 'Now, look at this.'

They'd halted in front of a window display where smiling mannequins displayed softly swirling skirts with boat-necked tops in feather-light knit fabric, or snug denim skirts with delicately ruched blouses.

'Mix and match,' Kirsten said. 'Get some decent jeans, two pairs of Capri pants, one denim and one white, a couple of skirts, half a dozen tops, and you can go anywhere, any time.'

She led Gabi inside, pausing just inside the door to grab a lightweight denim trench coat.

'Oh, isn't it to die for? Gabi, you simply must have this.'

'So you can borrow it?' Gabi teased, but she liked the coat, and knew it would look smart and be useful between seasons as she walked to and from work, though if she got the job at the new children's hospital she'd be driving to work...

'Hey, you should be smiling.' Kirsten must have caught her momentary hesitation. 'You don't *have* to buy the coat!'

'Oh, yes, I do,' Gabi told her, selecting the coat first and handing it to a saleswoman standing ready to ferry things to a changing room.

It was six o'clock before Gabi staggered home, laden with carry bags, lack of sleep adding to the hyped feeling in both her body and her brain.

'You shower and change into one of your new outfits,' Kirsten ordered, following Gabi into the flat with more parcels, packages and boxes. 'I called Alana earlier and she's free tonight, so we'll all go down to Mickey's for a drink then dinner to celebrate the new you. I'll even shout dinner.'

She whirled past Gabi, who'd paused in the small entry to the flat, her body tense as she tried to sense if Alex had returned.

'I'll dump these on the bed in the spare room,' Kirsten continued. 'That way, if you don't have time to unpack them all tonight, you'll still be able to get into your bed.'

Gabi watched as she disappeared into the spare bedroom, then saw her flip back out like a Jack-in-the-box, her eyes wide with astonishment.

'Gabi, there's a man asleep in your spare bedroom!' she said, whispering so loudly she could probably be heard on the ground floor. 'Is that what *this* is all about?'

She waved the goodies still slung across her arms to emphasise the 'this'.

'Of course it isn't,' Gabi told her, grabbing parcels from her and dumping them on an armchair. 'That's only Alex.

He's back to see his mother—flew in this morning, so I guess jet-lag caught up with him and he's come here to have a sleep.'

Then, concerned Kirsten might still believe she was changing her entire life because of Alex—of all men!—she added, 'This is about me, Kirsten, no one else.'

'Well, I'm glad,' Kirsten said, 'because I was reading just the other day where the women most likely to end up in a successful relationship are women who are self-focussed.'

Gabi rolled her eyes again.

'And where did *you* fit in this latest pop psychology quiz?'

'Oh, I'm a commitment-phile.' Kirsten seemed almost pleased with the label. 'I always think every man's ''the one'', then get shattered when it doesn't work that way. I had you down as the ''soul-mate'' type—you know, you think you've met your soul-mate, then you're disappointed because he doesn't match up to the ideal. Neither of us rank too well in the happy-ever-after stakes, but now you've switched to ''self-focussed'' you're on your way, girl!'

Kirsten gave her a high five by way of celebration, then wafted out the door, turning in the doorway to say, 'Seven at Mickey's, OK?' before crossing the small foyer to her own flat on the other side of the lift-well.

'Seven? That gives me exactly thirty minutes to shower, change and work out how to put on all the make-up I've just bought,' Gabi muttered to herself, but her thoughts were more on the person sleeping in her spare bedroom than the intricacies of make-up. Kirsten was right. She'd thought she'd found her soul-mate in Alex, way back when they'd been starting university. But apparently—and she'd proved it—soul-mates had little chance of success in their relationships.

She frowned as she picked up the parcels Kirsten had dumped.

Why?

Surely people who were alike in interest and outlook should have a good chance of maintaining a successful relationship.

She'd have to ask Kirsten, who, for all her ditzy ways, pop quizzes and flip talk, had an excellent brain hidden beneath the fashion-plate image. In fact, she'd completed her master's degree in psychology earlier in the year.

Dropping all the packages on the floor in the corner of her bedroom—she'd unpack properly tomorrow—Gabi searched through them for the white skirt with the aqua and gold beading around the hem and the matching aqua off-one-shoulder top. The outfit was sufficiently special for a celebration, which tonight definitely was, but not too dressy for Mickey's bar and bistro on the ground floor of the apartment block.

Once found, she spread the garments on the bed, dug through the bags again to find the pale blue bandeau Kirsten had insisted she could wear as a bra under the top—and the matching panties.

She smiled at the glamorous lingerie, and excitement kicked in again. The clothes might only be outward indications of her new self, but they were also the confidence boost she needed to stick to her plans.

Confidence which wavered slightly a little later as she opened the door to cross from bathroom to bedroom, clad only in the bandeau and briefs, and met a rumpled, sleep-dazed Alex peering uncertainly at her.

'What *are* you wearing?' he demanded.

'Underwear!' Gabi retorted, then, glancing at the faded black jocks stretched across his hips, she added, 'You?'

He obviously failed to see the humour in the situation, for he frowned, then growled, 'You're going out again? What about sleep? What kind of service do you think you'll give to patients if you're exhausted?'

Pleased she'd stirred him up enough to be grouchy, Gabi smiled.

'Terrible!' she told him. 'Really, really gross. So I'd better sleep tomorrow, hadn't I?'

She moved away into her bedroom, shutting the door so the pheromones couldn't follow and confuse her with issues that had nothing to do with her personal campaign of change. Though the scrunchy feeling in her stomach suggested they didn't need to follow—while Alex was around she'd find it impossible to *not* think of him.

Focus—that was what she needed.

The new clothes fitted beautifully, the white accentuating the tan on her freshly shaven and thoroughly moisturised legs. Aqua sandals—really nothing more than a few fine strips of leather—held together with a bow of glass beads—completed the outfit, and as Gabi twirled in front of the mirror a sense of excitement, so long missing from her life, filled her with the fizz of champagne bubbles.

'Toenails!'

The glitch was only momentary. She'd actually bought some new fast-drying nail polish a couple of weeks ago, though, as her toes rarely saw daylight, she hadn't bothered to use it. Slipping off the sandals, she applied the vibrant pink, knowing it would set while she did the make-up thing.

'I can do this!' she told herself as she opened little boxes and bottles and followed the procedure Luca's make-up girl had used.

'Boy! Even that worked! Maybe this transformation
aper's going to be a cinch.'

She twirled again, talking to herself in an effort to ignore
he voice that suggested maybe all this twirling stuff was
. way of putting off her exit from the room. An exit that
ould possibly—would probably—bring her into contact
vith Alex once again.

'Bulldust!' she muttered, but did a final twirl anyway,
hen, chin held high in what she hoped was a confident tilt
nd not a stiff-necked pose, she opened the door and
valked out.

After all, it was *her* flat—even if it was in Alex's name.

She wasn't sure whether to be glad or sorry when she
ound the living room deserted. Ditto the kitchen.

No way was she going to check the bathroom or second
edroom—it could give him the impression she cared
vhere he was. But she did feel slightly deflated.

Still, it was after seven—no time to brood; she had to
;o.

She grabbed her handbag then realised it didn't match.
Ruined the entire look. Surely they'd done handbags!

She thought back. A little aqua clutch—she remembered
Kirsten, high on spending someone else's money, throwing
t in with the shoe purchases.

Back into the bedroom, where she found the clutch,
ransferred money and handkerchief and the new, minimal
osmetics self-focussed women needed for touch-up jobs,
nd once again prepared to leave the flat.

Alex hadn't emerged from either bathroom or bedroom,
o Gabi called an obligatory goodbye in case he was still
n the flat and left, feeling new excitement as she heard the
ıp-tap of her stiletto heels click across the tiled foyer.

'Wow!'

Alana's reaction when she stepped into the lift on the

second floor was all Gabi could wish for, and though th
old Gabi might have uttered her thoughts—You don't thin
I've gone too far?—the new Gabi kept them inside an
savoured Alana's surprise.

'But you'll be wasted on Mickey's,' Alana continued
'Let's have a quick drink there then go on somewhere spe
cial—like the Blue Room. Somewhere people go to see an
be seen.'

They'd disembarked in the foyer and were walking to
wards the entrance to the bar and bistro, but before enterin
Gabi stopped and turned to the woman who'd been he
friend since they'd first met in kindergarten twenty-si
years earlier.

'I'm not doing this so I'll be seen—not for other people
Alana. I'm doing it for me. So I get the very most I ca
out of life. I'm doing it to make *me* feel good. I don'
believe anyone can "have it all", as the saying is thes
days, but I'm going to have a damn good go at having
whole lot more than I've been having.'

Alana eyed her doubtfully.

'I hear what you're saying but I'd find it a whole lo
easier to believe if Kirsten hadn't mentioned seeing Ale
asleep in your flat.'

Gabi exploded.

'This has nothing to do with any man!' she yelled at he
friend. 'Least of all Alex Graham, who's been out of m
life for far longer than the year we've been separated.'

She'd have stamped her foot as well, but remembered
just in time, the delicate stiletto heels on the new sandal
so made do with a fierce glare instead.

And just to make sure Alana let the subject drop, sh
repeated the main point.

'Alex Graham means nothing to me!'

'That's good,' Kirsten said, coming out of the bar—n

doubt, attracted by the yelling! 'Because the man I saw asleep on the bed is in there, having a drink with a willowy brunette. Diane someone, I think he said when he introduced her to Mickey.'

'Maybe we should go to the Blue Room—we can take a cab,' Alana suggested, but no matter how shaky her insides might be feeling, Gabi knew the new her had to go through with this, or the whole façade would crumble and she'd be back to being a colourless cipher before her campaign had properly started.

'Nonsense,' she replied, leading the way into the bar, pausing as she'd seen Kirsten sometimes do, just inside the door, so the foyer lights shone on her, spotlighting her entrance.

Then with long gliding steps, and praying the sandals didn't fall off, she moved towards the bar, eyes focussed on Mickey behind it so she didn't have to see who else was there.

The gleam of approval in his eyes boosted her flagging confidence.

'Can you do something aqua?' she asked, when he'd complimented her on her appearance. Mickey was owner of the bar and bistro but he preferred serving drinks to all other aspects of his job—maybe because it put him into the position of confidant to so many of the tenants. 'Something to match my top, but alcoholic as well.'

Mickey raised his eyebrows at this bold decision, coming from the least alcohol-tolerant of the three friends, but he made no comment. Though a growly noise from the far end of the bar, where two figures sat in relative gloom, gave Gabi an immense sense of satisfaction. She just hoped there was going to be enough alcohol in the drink Mickey produced to help her carry on this charade of disinterest.

But not so much she fell off her stool!

Though why should Alex's presence make her feel uneasy when she was, as she'd reminded Alana, long over him?

Kirsten and Alana had settled on stools on either side of her and now joined in the spirit of the evening, ordering outrageous cocktails.

'I wonder who else is off duty and not doing anything special,' Kirsten mused, when they'd toasted each other, tried each other's drinks and finally agreed on the CDs they wanted Mickey to stack.

The apartment block was home to mostly single and mostly medical people, who usually made up the main ingredients of an impromptu party in Mickey's bar.

Alana's eyes gleamed.

'We could have a party!'

'You can't have a party,' Mickey said, returning with an antipasto platter to set in front of them.

Alana wrapped him in her smile and murmured, 'Of course we can, Mickey, darling. We'll all be good. The last time wasn't our fault. It was those dentists caused the trouble. And to think His Nibs encouraged them to take that vacant flat because he thought they'd raise the tone of the place. As if we'd even *think* of wearing bedpans on our heads. In fact, I don't own one—and I can't remember ever nicking one, even in my student days.'

'I'm not talking about the last party—' Mickey began.

Kirsten said at the same moment, 'They were orthodontists, not dentists, and one of them was quite cute. In fact if I hadn't been so hung up over Josh, I might even have—'

'No party!' Mickey reiterated.

'Well, not a party but a few drinks,' Alana conceded. 'Pass us the phone, Mickey. Daisy will be working but I'll see who else is around. Anyone met the new guy on the third floor? Ingrid always scopes out the newcomers and

er comment was a roll of very expressive eyes and a long
wedish wolf whistle. Do Swedes have wolves that whis-
e?'

'Well, that rules him out of contention anyway,' Gabi
aid, not distracted by the question of whistling wolves. 'If
ngrid's got him in her sights, no one else stands a chance.
Vhy Her Highness employed a woman as gorgeous as
ngrid to be a nanny to the twins is beyond me! Talk about
utting temptation in His Nibs's way.'

'Ah, but His Nibs knows which side his bread's buttered
n,' Alana reminded her, slurping slush from the bottom of
er glass. 'Think of all he'd lose if he even thought about
quick fling with the nanny.'

Kirsten sipped at her drink and nodded.

'A precious bit of his anatomy for a start,' she said, and
ll three chuckled.

But Alana didn't get the phone, and the arrival shortly
fterwards of Graham and Madeleine Frost—unofficial
uilding managers by virtue of Madeleine's father owning
, and disrespectfully known to the friends as His Nibs and
Ier Highness—explained why Mickey had been so ada-
ant in refusing them a celebration in the bar.

'Private do, huh?' Alana asked him, but Mickey moved
way to the far side of the bar, which looked over the bistro
rea, without answering.

'Big brass with the Frosts,' Kirsten commented, and
Fabi nodded as she recognised several specialist consult-
nts and their wives or husbands in the group. But the sur-
rise came when Alex and his companion stood up and
valked around the bar to join the newcomers.

Gabi tried to rationalise it.

Alex and Graham had always been friendly. In fact, in
ne early days, as the only two married couples in the build-
ng, they'd often made up a foursome at dinner.

So it was natural he might join them.

And other hospital bigwigs?

A gnawing sense of disaster began in Gabi's gut and worked its way outward until she had to rub the goose bumps off her arms.

No, it couldn't be that he was back for good. He was here to see his mother—nothing more. After all, it was his determination to do his specialty studies overseas that had caused the problem even before she'd fallen pregnant. Then she'd wanted him to put his plans off, at least until she'd had the baby at home, with friends and family around her, but Alex had been adamant that they go.

'Hey! No brooding.' Kirsten's voice brought her out of the memories. 'Self-focussed people look ahead, not backwards.'

'What makes you think I'm looking backwards,' Gabi retorted. Ha! Self-focussed person standing up for herself. 'I was thinking we could have the party at my place. Mickey will send up pizzas. Let's go, girls. We can phone around from there.'

She just hoped when—she refused to consider an 'if'—Alex returned, the party would be so riotous he'd regret messing with her new life.

Hoped the party would be so riotous *she'd* forget the memories of the past his return had flung in her face.

Alex heard the noise as soon as he got out of the lift and hesitated, not for the first time regretting the impulse that had made him force the issue with Gabi and insist on staying in the flat.

Not that there had been any viable alternative. His mother would have been devastated if he'd stayed in a hotel because she'd have assumed, not without reason, given his behaviour earlier in her relationship with her new husband that he wouldn't stay at their old home because of Fred. But, in fact, it was Diane Kennedy's interest in him that made him steer clear of the place, an interest he didn't return but couldn't blatantly repulse, considering their step-relationship.

As if he didn't have enough complications in his life...

Tiredness tensed his gut and bunched the muscles in his shoulders but, from the noise, the good night's sleep he'd been hoping to get when he'd put Diane in a cab was as likely as his mother recovering from the chronic myelocytic leukaemia from which she was suffering. Though at present she was responding to treatment, so at least she had a temporary respite. He doubted he'd get even that.

He leant against the wall in the foyer, gathering strength before opening the door and plunging into the noise. Considering alternatives.

A hotel?

Without luggage? Not even a toothbrush?

Maybe he'd sleep through the noise—he was tired enough.

Damn it all, he needed sleep. How the hell could he decide what he was going to do next when he'd had about three hours' sleep in the last thirty-six?

At least tonight's informal conversation with Rod Griffiths, head of all the intensive care units at Royal Westside, had been encouraging. Should Alex decide to stay here, he'd be able to slot into a specialist programme in the new year—two months away.

If he decided to stay...

An image of Gabi as he'd seen her in the bar popped obligingly into his head.

Damn her, too. What the hell did she think she was playing at, going around in clothes like that?

And drinking cocktails, when she knew she didn't have a head for alcohol?

Dark anger he had no right to feel flared, propelling him across the foyer where he unlocked and pushed open the door. The wall of noise stopped him momentarily, then he recognised Alana among the revellers and, certain she must be behind the transformation of Gabi from a quiet, self-effacing person to the siren he'd seen in the bar, he strode towards her.

'Alex!' she said, acknowledging him with a smile and a nod of her head, but then ignoring his presence as she continued to dance with a youth who didn't look old enough to shave.

Alex looked around. Once Gabi knew he was back she'd turn down the music. But he couldn't see her, and his anger built again so when Alana, apparently deciding she'd ignored him long enough, tapped him on the shoulder, he spun towards her.

'Where is she?' he demanded.

'In the bathroom,' Alana said calmly.

Too calmly?

'But you'll never sleep with this racket going on,' Alana continued. 'Here's the key to my flat. Just leave the door on the latch so I can get in later. The spare bed's made up.'

He wanted to ask who she thought she was, giving him orders in his own flat, but even through the exhaustion and anger he was feeling he knew it wouldn't be fair. For all that his name was on the lease, it was Gabi who'd paid the rent for the last twelve months.

And if the Gabi he'd pictured when he'd made the decision to come home—the Gabi his friends had assured him had no new man in her life—no longer existed, then that was his problem.

He took the key, thanked Alana and headed for the second bedroom to retrieve some clean clothes and his toilet gear. The bathroom door *was* shut, but anyone could be in there. And the door to the main bedroom was shut as well.

It's none of your damn business where she is, who she's with or what she does, he reminded himself, but now his stomach muscles were as bunched as his shoulders, and he ached to hit someone—anyone—just for the pure physical release of the tension he was feeling.

CHAPTER THREE

'No! Who could be so inhuman as to put on music at this hour?' Gabi grumbled to herself, lifting an arm still weighed down with tiredness out from under the bedclothes so she could squint at her watch.

Three o'clock?

She could see, and the light wasn't on, so it was definitely daylight. Had she slept all day?

And what day would that be, pray tell?

The confusion, partnered by a dull ache behind her eyes and a voracious hunger, suggested she might have had one glass of wine too many the previous evening. She closed her eyes as the daylight made them smart.

Maybe two glasses too many the previous evening.

The previous evening...

She tried to piece it together.

Drinks at Mickey's—was blue alcohol more potent than other colours? Then a party in the flat. People had come from everywhere...

Had someone stayed over? Was that someone responsible for the noise in the kitchen?

Cautiously, she checked the other side of her wide queen-size bed. Totally unrumpled so, no, she hadn't done anything terminally stupid.

She pressed her hand against her forehead. There was definitely someone in the flat because she could smell coffee, and coffee seemed like a very good idea.

Coffee and aspirin.

Now!

She slithered out of bed and blearily pulled open the doors of her wardrobe, reaching her hand in for her old bathrobe which should have been on a hook at the far end. Feeling nothing, she forced her eyes to focus, then swore as a vast empty space met her eyes.

Someone had stolen all her clothes! Was the thief still in the flat?

Putting on music and making coffee?

She slapped her forehead at her own stupidity. 'I don't think so!'

Then, slowly, because she'd been exhausted by the time she'd fallen into bed and her sleep had been deeper than usual, memories of the events of the previous day returned. Packages and plastic bags stacked in the corner of the room reminded her of what she'd done, and she wasn't sure whether to be horrified at her behaviour or to laugh out loud.

All because of a needle-stick injury?

And no donor blood.

And six months of waiting before she'd know, though statistically the chances, even if the donor was positive, were so minimal as to almost not count.

She wouldn't think about that. Right now, the priority seemed to be clothes.

More memories returned. She'd bought a robe in the lingerie shop. A long black satin robe, rich with silk embroidery, including, if she remembered rightly, an image of a golden dragon standing upright on the back, his smiling head resting on one shoulder.

She shuffled through the bags, found the robe, shook it out and slipped into it. The cool material slid sensuously across her skin, making her feel like a million dollars. Well, half a million—there was still the headache. Across the hall for a quick teeth-clean and hair-brush—holy cow, had she really had her hair dyed in stripes? Then out to the kitchen to investigate the coffee. At this stage she was beyond caring who had made it—as long as they were willing to share.

'Alex?'

How the hell had she forgotten that part of yesterday's upheavals? It was coming back to her in flashes—Alex outside the flat, in Mickey's with Diane. She hadn't seen him after that...

Her eyes narrowed with suspicion as she wondered just where *he'd* spent the night.

Not that it was any of her business.

What *was* her business was hiding the stupid reaction of her body now it had realised just who was making coffee. It was nothing more than conditioning—like Pavlov's dogs salivating when bells rang.

Well, her days of salivating were over. The new Gabi was strong enough to ignore whatever physical demons Alex's presence could produce within her.

The silence had gone on long enough so she went for safety.

'How's your mother? Have you seen her today?'

He nodded.

'I spent a couple of hours there this morning. Fred came in to have lunch with her, so I left them alone.'

Gabi opened her mouth to suggest that spending more time with Fred *and* his mother—seeing them together— might help his relationship with Fred, but she remembered, just in time, that his relationship with Fred was also none of her business.

'Coffee?'

The suggestion was so welcome she couldn't help smiling at him.

'It's what brought me out here. Three o'clock! I've never slept this late.'

'You've never stayed awake so long after night duty,' Alex said, and Gabi had to use the raised-eyebrow thing again to remind him he no longer knew what she did or didn't do.

And, if the quick frown tugging his own eyebrows closer was any indication, he'd got the message. He poured her coffee and pushed the mug across the kitchen divider to where she'd perched on a stool.

Silence pressed around them once again, growing thicker by the minute and threaded with old-familiar-type signals, and, on her side at least, the wretched Pavlovian responses. She had to break the tension before it strangled her.

'So, how was Scotland?'

Oh, please! Couldn't she do better than that?

'Cold and wet when I left.'

Something in his voice suggested this had been more the norm than otherwise and, knowing how much he loved being outdoors, she had to ask.

'Doesn't sound like your kind of place. Though surely you'd looked into the weather patterns before you chose Edinburgh. Was it anything like you'd expected, or were you disappointed?'

'The hospital and work itself was great, and on good weekends there's fantastic walking in the hills or along the coastline. You can take a train an hour's journey from the city—in any direction—and be in beautiful country, Gabi.'

He meant it, and she knew he'd have enjoyed the explorations, but there was something else in his voice which suggested it hadn't all been sheer joy.

'Were you homesick?'

He looked startled, then his dark eyes scanned her face, as if trying to read a hidden message there. And did the shrug mean he hadn't found it—or that he found the question too stupid to answer?

'I'm staying home.' The words came out so abruptly they gave the impression they'd escaped without him meaning them to.

So abruptly that Gabi was confused.

'You mean you're shifting over to your mother's place?' She felt relieved and guilty all at once. Guilt won. 'You don't have to. You can stay here. After all, it won't be for long.'

Wrong answer?

From the way he was frowning now, maybe she'd misheard the question—though it hadn't really been a question, had it?

She tightened the sash on the beautiful robe because, now she considered it, the frown seemed to be directed towards her cleavage, which looked OK from where she sat but might have been gaping from Alex's side of the divider.

'I mean I'm staying here for good—I'm not going back to Scotland. Well, not in the foreseeable future.'

The words shocked Gabi so much she almost stuttered, finally managing to get out, 'Have you spoken to your mother's doctor? Is she worse than they'd previously thought? I know a cure's unlikely, but I thought...I assumed...'

'She could live for years? Of course she could—and hopefully she will.'

'So why come home?' Gabi demanded.

What she really meant was why barge in and mess up her life—again—just when she was finally getting sorted. But saying that might give him satisfaction. Self-focussed women played it cool.

Alex's shrug suggested he didn't have an answer, but Alex was a planner—not a spur-of-the-moment man—so he had an answer all right. He just wasn't going to share it.

Diane popped obligingly into Gabi's head.

As if you care, she reminded herself, then realised Alex was talking again. Something about Rod Griffiths, a job at Royal Westside, accommodation, staying here.

'Staying here? In this flat? With me?'

Bloody hell, she sounded more hysterical than cool, and Alex was doing the shrugging thing again. *Definitely* something going on!

'You just said I could,' Alex reminded her.

'That was when I thought you'd be here a week or so,' she snapped. 'Anyway, why would you want to stay here if it's for longer?'

'It's handy to the hospital. And I don't mean for ever, just until I find somewhere else.'

It was on the tip of his tongue to remind her, again, that the flat was in his name, but caution prevailed. He sensed Gabi was already floundering and he didn't want to push her so far she ordered him out.

He was floundering a bit himself. It had to be the black thing she was wearing, with a damn dragon, of all things, peering slyly at him over her shoulder. His gaze kept straying back to it, which made it impossible for him not to look at the pale skin revealed between the flower-encrusted lapels.

Pale skin reflecting the colour of those flowers and hinting, with its light and shadows, at the fullness of the breasts imperfectly concealed.

'If that's OK with you.'

She looked as if it was anything but OK with her, but as he felt he didn't know this woman with hair that looked as if the sun was shining through it and a shimmery, sexy black gown replacing the old bathrobe he remembered, he really couldn't guess at her thoughts.

'If it's convenience you want, you could just as easily stay at Alana's. In her spare bedroom.'

He frowned at the suggestion. Why didn't she want him staying here?

Were the friends who claimed she wasn't seeing anyone wrong?

Not knowing made him more determined to dig in his heels.

'I spent last night there—the bed's atrocious and there's some stupid bloody bird that starts talking as soon as dawn breaks.'

'You spent last night at Alana's?'

Hah! Got her there!

'She offered me her key. I was bushed and not likely to get much sleep with the noise your guests were making.'

'And where was I while you and Alana were making these arrangements?'

He tried to analyse her tone, but she pushed her coffee-cup away as she spoke and the gown fell a little more open, distracting him with memories of the feel of those soft breasts.

Determined not to be diverted—or attracted—he focussed on recalling the events of the previous evening, and remembered his doubts.

'In the bathroom—or so Alana said.'

Gold-flecked hazel eyes lifted to study him—stared into his.

'So Alana said?' she repeated softly, and it wasn't hard to analyse her tone this time. Pure steel, that was what it was. 'If that's what she said, where *else* would I have been?'

He shrugged, as if it wasn't important, but he was suddenly aware he was balancing on a knife-edge as far as Gabi was concerned. One false move and he'd be out of his flat so fast he'd leave skid marks on the carpet.

'You could have been anywhere—it was none of my business.' He hurried the words, anxious for this not to escalate into an argument.

'Good!' She nodded. 'Just as long as you remember that!'

Gabi laying down the law?

His Gabi telling him his place?

Only she wasn't his Gabi any more.

The reminder made him stand up, collecting both their cups and turning to rinse them at the sink. The follow-up thought—she'd damned well better not be anyone else's—had jolted him so much movement had been a necessity.

He cast a quick glance over his shoulder. She, too, had moved and was walking, the dragon swaying seductively across her back, towards the CD player. Would she change the music? He'd put on an old heavy metal CD he'd bought early in their marriage—one she'd never really liked.

Had he chosen it deliberately?

Now he was shrugging at his own questions. He didn't think so, though he hadn't given it much thought, had just sorted through the stack, noticed it and put it on.

She didn't change it, just lowered the volume slightly, then turned to smile at him.

'It was a trifle loud.' The words could have been an apology for her actions, but he was so stirred up—in many ways—he took them as criticism.

'Planning on going back to bed, were you?' he said, the roughness in his voice startling him as well as making her hesitate as she crossed the living room.

'No, actually I'm not, but I know Kirsten—she's new since you left, she's in the flat across the hall—was up even later than I was, because she went out clubbing after she left here. So she might still be sleeping. I'm going out.'

And, on what she felt was an excellent exit line, Gabi left the room. She hadn't really intended going out, and there was no way she should let Alex's presence dictate her comings and goings, but if she stayed in the flat for any longer than it would take her to shower and dress she'd go screaming mad.

Once in her bedroom, she stared at the as yet unopened packages.

She should hang up the clothes, put away the other things—but that meant staying in the flat. What she really should do was tell Alex to get lost—that this was her space now and she didn't want him in it. But apparently the self-focus thing didn't extend to ordering ex-husbands around. Well, not at this early stage of it, anyway.

So she'd go out. In fact, she'd go up and visit his mother. While Fred was there, it was one place Alex wouldn't be.

She rifled through the bags until she found the white Capri pants. Fortunately, like most of the things Kirsten had insisted she buy, they were a non-iron fabric so hadn't suffered from sitting in their bag on the floor all night.

She'd team them with the red vest top and the white cardigan. According to Kirsten, a woman couldn't have too many cardigans, though, as Gabi remembered the number Kirsten had added to her pile of purchases, she did wonder.

The fashion guru had decreed white Lycra undies for this particular outfit, the material splashed with red flowers. Determined not to be caught, again, in her underwear, Gabi took all the clothes with her to the bathroom. Took the make-up bag as well—the light was much better in there and, though she wouldn't need much, she needed the practice in getting it right.

Alex's double-take as she waltzed into the living room

a little later made it all worthwhile. The new bra gave her bustline a terrific boost and the figure-hugging material of the trousers emphasised the swell of her hips in a good way rather than a bad, while cheeky white sandals made her ankles look slimmer and, to her own critical eyes, her legs look longer.

'I don't know when I'll be back,' she said. Actually, visiting Jane Kennedy would only take an hour at most, but there was something very liberating about saying 'I don't know when I'll be back' to Alex. She could understand what women meant when they talked about empowerment.

He didn't reply, but the way his gaze travelled over her body warmed her skin and made the flesh beneath it tremble with remembered desire.

Not exactly the moment for sex to be rearing its head—after more than twelve months of dormancy.

'There's a bit of food in the fridge,' she said, to make walking out on him feel a bit easier. Then she remembered they hadn't resolved the issue of him staying in the flat.

Not that she had any intention of mentioning it right now. She'd think about it later. Perhaps, during her hospital visit, she could find out if Diane was still living at her father's and stepmother's home.

It wasn't that Gabi cared what went on between Alex and Diane, she assured herself as she began walking, again taking a different route—she just didn't see any reason to actually throw them together.

But if Alex stayed on in the flat he'd realise that, for all her new clothes and streaky hair, she was still as unattached as she'd been when he'd departed.

What she needed was a man. Not necessarily a great affair—or even a small affair—just a man who'd look as if he was interested in her, pop around now and then, give Alex the impression he was a fixture in her life.

The intern was too young, and Ned Blacklock, who'd been pestering her to go out with him since Alex had taken off for Scotland, was too serious. He'd think his persistence had paid off if she suddenly began to accept his invitations. And, because he was a nice guy, she didn't want to do anything that might eventually hurt him.

There was always Josh, Kirsten's ex-boyfriend. Scared-of-commitment Josh, they'd named him. He was just the man!

Thinking of Josh, who was a paediatric specialist at the hospital, should have reminded her of her list but instead the name of Rod Griffiths, another specialist, bobbed into her head. What had Alex said about Rod? About a job?

Rod Griffiths was in overall charge of the staffing of the coronary care unit, the burns unit and the general intensive care unit at the hospital, and thus decided who fitted the intensivist specialty training programme and who didn't. But slotting someone into a training programme with only two months left of the year seemed unlikely. In fact, the only place always in need of doctors, and constantly taking on temporary staff from an agency, was A and E—which was also the natural stepping-stone for Intensive Care.

No! Fate might have brought Alex back into her life—temporarily—but surely it wouldn't be so capricious as to set him down in her department.

Though, if he did start there, he'd be on a different team. Need she see him?

She reminded herself of the list and her new focus in life—and the sooner she could get a rotation to Paediatrics the better—but uncertainty was unravelling her determination, while memories of her body's reaction to Alex's presence were eroding her confidence in her ability to change her life.

She'd reached the hospital and determinedly put all the uncertainty behind her as she took the lift up to the oncology unit, pausing to speak to the nurse on duty at the nurses' station.

'Mrs Kennedy's like a new woman since her son came back,' the nurse said. 'And no wonder. He's so nice—and so good-looking, isn't he? And wouldn't it be romantic if he and Mr Kennedy's daughter were to get together?'

Gabi clamped her lips tightly together, though as she made her way to Jane's room she muttered to herself about gushing, gossipy staff, and was still muttering as she pushed open the door.

'Gabi! I was wondering if you'd come.'

Jane's greeting was as warm as ever, and Gabi crossed to the bed to kiss the woman she thought of as a second mother.

'Of course I'd come,' she protested.

Probably overdoing it, because Jane chuckled then murmured, 'Just not when the grouch was here!'

The words shocked Gabi—not the assumption that she and Alex couldn't be together, but 'the grouch' name Jane had used. She'd first used it when she'd started seeing Fred Kennedy, and Alex, still not properly over his father's death, had found his mother's new relationship hard to handle. And though both Jane and Gabi had tried to talk to him about it he'd retreated into grouch-like silence on the subject rather than discussing his feelings openly.

Surely his mother didn't still see him that way?

'I guess you know he's staying at the flat,' Gabi said.

Jane nodded.

'If you don't mind having him until he finds somewhere of his own, I'd be grateful. Poor Fred's not coping too well

with my illness, and Diane's shifted in, supposedly to look
after him, but she's about as much use as a head cold.'

'But far more attractive,' Gabi reminded her, and they
both laughed.

The door behind her opened again and, expecting to see
Fred, Gabi turned, a smile of welcome on her face.

Alex knew, the moment he saw it fade, that the smile
hadn't been meant for him, but seeing it, seeing Gabi's face
light up in the special way it always had when she smiled,
had wrenched at something inside his chest.

Walking out again was his preferred option, but the smile
on his mother's face was of genuine delight, and he didn't
want to see it disappear as well. He crossed to the bed and
kissed her on the cheek, then settled on the far side, across
from Gabi in her tight white pants and cheeky red top and
her shining, sunshiny hair.

'So, both my children visiting me at once,' his mother
said, and Alex winced at the reminder of how close his
mother had been to Gabi. And how wonderful Gabi had
been when his father had died.

While he'd retreated into a haze of shock and misery,
Gabi had helped his mother through those first few terrible
months, always there for her. So much so he'd felt resentment, although he knew she'd have been his support as
well—had he let her. But it had been Gabi siding with his
mother later, actually telling him he should try to understand why she needed someone like Fred, that had accel-
erated the trouble between them. Then Gabi accusing him,
by choosing Scotland to specialise, of running away from
his problems with his mother, rather than sorting them
out...

'You're supposed to contribute to the conversation.'

His mother's comment brought him back to the present.

'I was saying how much I like Gabi's hair this way. I

envy young people today. They've got so many choices, even in things like hair colour, and the confidence to get out there and try something different.'

'The choices are there for everyone,' Gabi reminded her. 'Surely it's never too late to grasp at opportunities, or to choose to change. Let's take hair colour as an example. Did you ever want to be blonde, or maybe a redhead—any colour you'd fancy for a change?'

Alex found the conversation hard to believe. His mother and Gabi discussing hair colours! In all the years he'd known Gabi—twelve?—he'd never known her take more than a passing interest in her personal appearance, while as for his mother...

'A really dark purple,' his maternal relative was now saying as he tuned back in. 'Like black, but with purple lights rather than red or blue ones.'

'You want purple hair? Mum, you're nearly sixty!' The protest was out before he could stop it.

'I'm fifty-six,' she said with dignity. 'And if that's not reason enough to have purple hair, I don't know what is.'

'Way to go, Jane!' Gabi said, clapping as if his mother had done something clever. 'And if you find you don't like purple, you can always go blonde. I think you'd make a sensational blonde, with your dark eyes and olive skin. You know, like those northern Italian blondes. Beautiful!'

Alex found himself wishing Fred would walk in—maybe then the conversation would swing back to the realms of the believable. What had happened to discussions of books, or television documentaries, or the state of the world?

Maybe he could start one.

It would certainly be better than listening to prattle about purple hair.

'Are you reading anything interesting at the moment, Mum?'

'Well, I've just finished the Harry Potter series—'

'Harry Potter? They're kids' books, aren't they?'

'Yes, but adults enjoy them,' his mother replied with the kind of mild reproof in her voice that set his teeth on edge. 'Actually, Gabi lent them to me, and I enjoyed them so much I asked Fred to bring in a pile of my old books. Things *I* read in my childhood. I wanted to compare them. He brought some of your old Dungeons and Dragons books as well—they're not so different.'

He should have stuck with the hair conversation, as the idea of both his mother, who usually read biographies and autobiographies, and his ex-wife, whose tastes ran to crime and mysteries, reading children's books was so bizarre he felt set adrift from reality.

'We actually went to a medieval fair not so long ago,' his mother continued. 'Gabi and I—Fred didn't come, witches and wizards aren't really his thing—but Gabi had heard they usually have booths and discussion groups at medieval celebrations.'

Understanding dawned. His mother, shocked by the diagnosis of her condition, had turned to so-called miracle workers.

'Mum,' he said, speaking gently, 'although your kind of leukaemia can't be cured, regular medical treatment will keep you alive for a long time. You don't need potions or witches' brews.'

Gabi's laughter filled the room.

'Oh, dear,' his mother said, though she, too, was chuckling. 'I'm sorry. You must have thought I was mad. Of course I didn't go for witches' brews or magic potions. We went to look and to meet and talk to people who believe they have special powers, and to listen to what they had to say. We went because we thought it would be fun, and it jolly well was, wasn't it, Gabi?'

Gabi nodded her agreement and wiped tears of laughter from her eyes.

'Maybe we should have taken some of the lessons they were offering,' she said to Jane. 'Then we could have zapped this disbeliever into the next century.'

Jane eyed her son.

'I don't know,' she said to Gabi, her lips twitching as she tried not to smile. 'I think he might have been happier in the last one.'

'Or even further back,' Gabi suggested. 'Perhaps a troglodyte.'

'I hope that's not me you're discussing,' a voice said, and she turned to see Fred come through the door, with Diane close behind him.

'What's a troglodyte?' Diane asked.

And before Gabi could reply, or even decide if she wanted to, Jane slipped in a teasing, 'Alex.'

But to Gabi it seemed the light-hearted atmosphere had changed into something more sober and she could feel tension again stiffening the air.

'I think you've got more than enough visitors,' she said to Jane, and she stood up, leaned over to kiss the older woman goodbye then, with a general farewell to the others, left the room.

Alex caught up with her as she waited for the lift.

'So I'm a troglodyte, am I?' he growled.

'I didn't say that—your mother did,' Gabi reminded him.

'You started it,' Alex argued as the lift doors swung open. He stood back while she entered, then followed close behind her.

Too close.

'Do you know what the word means? Do you actually know what a troglodyte is?' he asked, his voice still deep and gruff.

Gabi hesitated a moment too long, giving him the chance to answer his own question.

'He's a caveman, Gabi,' he said softly, standing very close to her and speaking so only she could hear, although the lift was stopping on every floor and more and more people were getting in. 'And do you know what a troglodyte did when he fancied a woman? He threw her over his shoulder and carried her back to his cave, where he flung her down onto a soft pile of animal skins and had his wicked way with her.'

The words, together with his closeness, generated so much heat within Gabi she wondered about spontaneous combustion, and when Alex added, 'Probably more than once,' she thought her bones would melt.

But she knew he was only teasing her, giving her a little of her own back after she and his mother had teased him. Alex had been gone for twelve months, but months before that he'd lost interest in her as a woman, so letting herself be seduced by his words would only bring on the pain and misery of frustration she'd suffered in the last months of their marriage.

The lift had reached the ground floor, and she followed the rest of the disembarking passengers out into the hospital foyer. She just hoped she wasn't as red as her top.

'I'm popping into A and E to have a look around,' Alex said in his normal voice, not the throaty, spine-tingling one he'd used in the lift. 'See what's changed since I was last there so I don't make too many mistakes tomorrow.'

Tomorrow!

Gabi raised her eyes to heaven—she'd been right about malign fates. Though having Alex working in the same department would make her push much harder for a transfer to Paediatrics. However, right now she had to change her plans for keeping out of his way. She'd been going to duck into A and E herself, not to check out the area but to tidy up some paperwork she'd left undone the previous morning.

Now that he was going there it wouldn't work. So she said casually, 'See you later.' And tried to block images of cave entrances and piles of thick animal skins out of her mind as she walked away from him.

Once outside the hospital, her feet turned automatically to the right, following the old familiar route home. At least, as she could have walked it blindfolded, she could think and walk, and not feel obliged to look around her.

OK! So she'd blocked out the cave and pile of animal skins, but could she continue to block other things out of her mind if Alex stayed on at the flat? Could she maintain the focus she'd need to change her life, or would she slide back into the welter of doubt and confusion that had begun earlier but had deepened when she'd first been pregnant and had discovered her joy at this admittedly badly timed mistake had not been shared by Alex.

Maybe Kirsten's pop psychology was right. She was a 'soul-mate' type and, thinking she'd found her perfect match, someone who shared every facet of her life, she'd been shattered as much by the realisation of her misconceptions as she had by Alex's reaction.

Death of a soul-mate! It would make a moody country-and-western-type song. But Alex hadn't died, he'd just shown himself to be human, with needs and a focus that didn't fit with hers after all.

For the first time she realised what a great part her disappointment in the person she'd thought Alex to be had played in their estrangement. And when she looked at it like that the burden was all hers, because Alex had never pretended to be anything other than what—or who—he was.

A sudden screech of car tyres pulled her out of the useless speculation, and she stepped back onto the kerb as Josh Phillips pulled up in front of her and climbed out over the door of his classy black convertible.

'Gabi! I thought it was you. What on earth are you doing, woman? Trying to commit suicide? If I wasn't such a great driver you'd be raspberry jam beneath my wheels by now.'

Gabi grinned at him. For all his lack of commitment in relationships it was hard not to like Josh, who was a top-class paediatrician and totally committed to the children in his care.

'I was thinking, but I'm sure I looked before stepping off the kerb. I bet you came around that corner far too fast.'

'Like the wind!' Josh admitted, then he flipped her hair.

'Love the new look,' he said, his blue eyes travelling admiringly up and down her body. 'Surely you're not doing anything boring, like going home, when you should be being seen somewhere special.'

'I *was* on my way home,' Gabi admitted, 'but I'd been thinking about you earlier. There's something I wanted to ask you. Have you time for a coffee, or a drink somewhere?'

'You have but to command and my steed awaits you!' he declared, executing a sweeping bow towards his car. 'I *do* have to call at the hospital, but I'll only be a couple of minutes. Then we might try that new wine bar on the river. That suit you?'

Gabi nodded, then looked dubiously at the little sports car, not sure about the mechanics of climbing in.

Josh must have sensed her hesitation.

'For you, I open the door!' he said, doing the job with a flourish. 'Now, a scarf for that beautiful hair.'

He dug in the glove box and produced a patterned scarf Gabi recognised as Kirsten's.

She took it without comment, though she wondered how someone who longed for commitment as much as Kirsten did could have fallen for a flirt like Josh.

He continued to chat as they drove around the corner to the hospital, where he pulled up right outside the front doors and with a 'Back in a tick' leapt out, again over his door, and disappeared through the automatic doors.

But it wasn't Josh walking in that Gabi saw as the doors opened, but Alex walking out.

Maybe the fates weren't so malign after all.

CHAPTER FOUR

A DRINK led to dinner but, though Josh flirted outrageously, Gabi knew it was just his way and played along, pleased by the fact he seemed to think her chances of getting a short stint on the paediatric ward were good.

'There's always someone going off on holidays or to a conference, and the place, like most of the hospital, is usually understaffed. It might take a week or two to work out, and longer before they can slot you in, but I'll let you know.'

Though she'd expected it, at the mention of the delay Gabi's heart sank; then she reminded herself that A and E was usually so busy she wouldn't have time to be bothered by Alex.

Declining Josh's invitation to go dancing—'Look at me! I'm hardly dressed for it'—she agreed to a lift home, firmly ending the evening by mastering the 'getting out of the car without opening the door' technique in front of the apartment building, then turning to thank him and say goodbye.

She handed him back the scarf, and saw the way he glanced up at Kirsten's window.

Was the flirt ready to change his ways?

That's for Kirsten to find out, she told herself, but in the meantime Josh had had his uses. She unlocked her door and pushed it open, listening for noises that might tell her if Alex was in or not. No TV blaring, no hard rock music—curiosity warred with relief.

Well, she hoped it was curiosity, and not the more sinister, green-eyed dragon of jealousy.

66

Either way, she was really too tired to care, so she made her way to bed. Surely, after a proper night's sleep, she'd be able to think rationally about Alex's return and work out how to cope with it—both at home and at work. The 'at work' thing was beyond her control, but she didn't have to give in to his assumption that he could stay on in the flat.

She closed her eyes and tried to think of other things—then remembered the bags still stacked neatly in the corner of the room. *She* could move out. After all, she was already packed, and she'd slept in Alana's spare bed often enough to know where the broken spring was and how to curl her body around it.

And she was already packed.

More or less.

Some time during an internal debate on the wisdom or otherwise of this course, and whether moving out diminished or enhanced self-focus, she fell asleep, waking again to the smell of coffee and the sound of music. Only this time she was in no doubt as to whom it was in her kitchen, and she curled into a ball and hugged herself hard as a rush of longing so strong it took her breath away held her hostage.

If only she could turn back time…

But how far? Further than one year, that was for sure. Two? Would that be far enough, or had she and Alex already begun to drift apart even then?

Anyway, such speculation was useless. *And* she was going to be late for work if she didn't move right now! She hauled herself out of bed and rustled through the plastic bags, sure she must have bought some 'going to work' clothes.

Ha! Denim skirt with a demure split to just above her knees, pale blue T-shirt with a splashy red hibiscus on the front. Underwear? She hadn't time to sort through it for what Kirsten had considered appropriate so grabbed the first set that came to hand. Very lacy, but they'd have to do. She grinned as she admitted to herself that wearing sexy underwear *did*, as Kirsten had promised, make her feel special.

She managed the return journey to and from the bathroom without seeing Alex, though noises from the kitchen as she came out suggested he was still in the flat.

'Are you going to eat before you go to work, or is eating, like sleeping, something else you no longer consider important?'

He was definitely still in the flat, and if this kept up her attempt at self-focus would be trampled to death before she'd had a chance to get properly started.

Ignoring him was the only possible answer.

Back in her room, she grabbed her usual handbag, pleased to see it matched the tan sneakers she'd chosen to wear with today's outfit.

'I have a date with a Danish pastry in the canteen,' she said, trying to sound as casual as possible, though seeing Alex, dressed for work in serviceable jeans and crisp white shirt, made casual very difficult.

In fact, it made breathing very difficult.

With a garbled sound she hoped might sound like 'goodbye', or perhaps 'see you later', she hurried out the door, only to find, as she waited for the lift, that he was also ready to go. Which meant walking to work together. More memories, more breathing problems. It was too late, if she wanted breakfast, to take a different route, and she could hardly walk on the other side of the road.

Surely self-focussed people should be more confident than this! The lift doors slid closed and her nerves tightened as she remembered the words he'd spoken in another lift just yesterday.

But today he stood in stony silence and somehow that was worse. Fortunately, Alana got in on the second floor and, after flicking an admiring glance over Gabi's outfit and winking at her, she greeted Alex and demanded to know where he was off to so early.

'I'm sure A and E will be pleased to have you,' Alana said, though the look she shot Gabi was filled with sympathy. 'I'm still in Eight B,' she added, in response to Alex's question about her work. 'And likely to be there until I either retire or drop dead from shock because one of the specialists arrives on time.'

As they all headed towards the hospital, Alana continued to chat about the problems of running the hospital's admission ward, while Gabi, seeking distraction from thoughts of Alex, considered her friend.

Alana was confident, passionate about her work, a regular at the gym and a first-class tennis player who still played fixtures. She had theatre tickets for the first night of every new production at the State Theatre, a great social life and to all intents and purposes perfectly fitted the description of a self-focussed woman which Kirsten had detailed for Gabi's benefit on Saturday.

So, statistically, she should be one of the people who'd found happiness with someone.

'And, statistically, you should have your head examined for even considering the secondhand version of some couch potato's psychoanalysis!'

'Was that something you want to share, or were you talking to yourself?' Alana asked, turning back at the staff entrance to wait for Gabi to catch up.

'Just telling myself how stupid I am to be even thinking about the latest of Kirsten's ''perfect match'' theories.'

Gabi looked around, wondering where Alex had gone and when.

'Into A and E and some time ago,' Alana told her when Gabi wondered aloud. 'He said he wanted to be early so he could meet the team, but that you're having breakfast before you start. I'll join you for a coffee. Sue Croft is coming off duty, and if I'm late enough she'll deliver the handover report to someone else and I won't have to listen to how hard it is to work on Eight.'

Gabi smiled because listening to Alana's usual complaint reassured her that the world was twirling properly on its axis and, although one of them might have begun a personal transformation, nothing would ever affect their friendship.

Speaking of which...

'I wondered if I might shift in with you for a few weeks—just until Alex finds somewhere to live.'

She met Alana's querying look with a slight shrug.

'It's uncomfortable,' she added, by way of explanation.

Alana grinned at her.

'That I *can* believe! Actually, it would really suit me if you did. I've been offered the chance to do a course down in Melbourne. It's a last-minute opportunity as someone else pulled out, and I'm leaving in the morning. I was going to ask you to look after my menagerie. If you're living there it won't be as much hassle for you.'

They chatted on as they finished their coffee, both carefully avoiding the subject of Alex's return. Gabi knew Alana would always be there to listen to her if she needed to talk, but she wouldn't ask questions or offer unasked-for advice. Though she did give Gabi's cheek a quick kiss as they parted near the canteen door.

'Hang in there,' she said quietly. 'You'll sort it all out in the end.'

Would she?

The question went unanswered as she arrived in A and
E to find ambulances decanting people injured in a pile-up
on one of the commuter ring-roads.

'Nothing really serious,' Roz told her, 'but it's all hands
on deck while everyone's checked out. Paul Canty's team
is on the swing shift and he's suggested we keep any doubtful ones down here for observation, rather than admitting
them to a ward. They're mostly green, though Paul is in
with a yellow at the moment.'

Gabi understood Roz's comment, though to an outsider
she might have been talking about green and yellow people.
An internationally accepted coding system prioritised patients, and green meant a patient had localised injuries with
no obvious threat to any system or injury that might cause
loss of life or limb. A green patient could wait for treatment
for several hours.

A yellow was next best from the patient's point of view.
He or she might have more serious injuries but could tol-
erate a wait of up to an hour. A yellow would always be
seen before a green.

'Could you take the woman who's up the end? She's not
badly injured, but pregnant and upset.'

Gabi made her way to the cubicle Roz indicated, where
a pregnant woman in an advanced state of hysterics made
Roz's description of 'upset' laughable.

'But you don't know it hasn't harmed the baby,' the
woman was yelling. 'I want an ultrasound and I want it
now, and I want to see my specialist. He comes to this
hospital; I know he does.'

Gabi glanced towards the nurse, who obligingly filled her
in.

'We put a foetal heart monitor on her as soon as she

came in. You can see the baby's heartbeat's strong—perfectly normal.'

'That doesn't mean it mightn't have a broken leg or arm,' the woman yelled, and Gabi, knowing exactly how the patient must be feeling, moved towards the gurney and took her hand.

'We'll contact your specialist. It's better if he does the ultrasound because he'll have other images for comparison.'

She nodded to a nurse who held the patient file, and as the young man departed to call the specialist Gabi smoothed the woman's tangled hair back from her forehead.

'For the moment let's assume, because he's not showing any signs of distress, that the baby's fine. After all, you've got a lot of fluid sloshing around in there to keep him cushioned from any bump. It's as if he has his very own air-bag.'

The woman looked at her as if she were mad, but at least she'd stopped wailing and the cessation of noise eased everyone's nerves.

'I need to examine you—to make sure you're OK. After all, you're the most important part of this pregnancy at the moment. Without you, that little one in there would have no hope of survival. Or not much. You're what? Thirty weeks?'

'Twenty-eight.'

Too soon for junior to be arriving, Gabi thought as she examined the woman for injuries, asking about the accident, where she'd been in the car, where the seat belt had been, relying on the woman's answers to give her some idea of where injuries might have occurred.

According to the patient, she'd been a passenger in a car driven by her husband and, though jolted forward when the car behind them had struck and shunted them into the stationary one in front of theirs, she hadn't hit any part of her body against the dash.

The nurse returned with the information that the obstetrician would be at the hospital to do his rounds within an hour and would see the A and E patient first.

Gabi explained to the woman that they'd keep her until he arrived, then left, wondering if self-focus was all that good. Except when she'd said he'd been driving the car the woman hadn't mentioned her husband, or asked for him.

An uneasiness in her own stomach suggested that either the Danish had been off—unlikely when they delivered fresh each morning—or memories of her own behaviour were tightening her intestines.

Running into Alex as she passed the desk didn't help.

Admittedly, after her own miscarriage she'd shut herself off from his sympathy—from him—but that had been because she'd known he hadn't wanted the baby. Surely that was different.

'I've a male, thirty-three, in four. He looked OK when he came in and responded to questions, but is now showing all the classic symptoms of shock,' Alex said. 'Could you take a look at him?'

Gabi accompanied him back to the cubicle, and her eyes took in the measures already in place to counteract shock. Fluid was running into the patient's arm in an effort to expand his blood volume, and monitors showed his heartbeat was steady, but the man was sweating profusely and shivering at the same time, and Gabi knew, without feeling him, that his extremities would be cold and his skin clammy to the touch.

A mask over his nose was ensuring a higher than usual concentration of oxygen was flowing into his lungs and another screen showed good oxygenation in his blood.

'You've got everything happening to stabilise him,' Gabi said, moving back towards the curtain so she could speak to Alex without upsetting the patient. 'What's worrying you?'

'The cause. He came in because he'd been knocked out—hit his head against the windscreen in spite of his seat belt. That means his chest *must* have struck the steering-wheel. Heaven knows, we see it often enough to be aware that kind of injury can result in a tear in the aorta or in some other vessel and internal bleeding would explain the shock, but there's no sign of blood loss in his BP. I've booked him for a CT scan just in case but, in the meantime, have you any suggestions?'

'Delayed shock isn't that uncommon,' Gabi said, fighting the *déjà vu* of working A and E again with Alex. The pregnant woman had obviously awoken a lot of buried memories. 'Have you talked to him? I realise you must have when you asked him where it hurt—but have you *really* talked to him? Perhaps he had a child in the car and is only now realising just how close they came to being seriously injured.'

Alex nodded.

'I guess it's possible, but you'd think there'd have to be a physical reason as well.'

'Not necessarily,' Gabi told him. 'I show all the symptoms of shock every time I think about going up in a plane—and that's not physical. Well, the symptoms are but the reason isn't.'

Gabi left him to it, moving on to the next patient, but the plane part of her conversation had reminded her about the rescue course. Was it too late to back out?

Did she need *that* much change in her life?

Especially now Alex was back and, should she want to,

she could discuss what had gone on with their marriage without ever setting foot in an aircraft.

We're not talking Alex here, she berated herself. We're talking change and whether she needed it.

Simple answer? Yes!

More complex answer? Still yes, because, if nothing else, keeping busy for the next six months would stop her brooding over that faint possibility of HIV. After all, no matter how low the odds, someone had to contract HIV from needle-stick injuries to make up the statistical point five of one per cent.

The day fell into its normal routine. The accident victims who'd been kept in were shifted to the corridor, still being observed but releasing curtained cubicles for new patients. Gabi was switched to the walking wounded, people who'd come by themselves or with relatives, needing attention ranging from suturing of minor wounds to hospitalisation for acute appendicitis.

She snatched a cup of tea at one stage and caught a glimpse of Alex disappearing behind a green curtain but, as she'd guessed, their paths rarely crossed. Until a young girl who'd slashed her wrists was brought in, with such serious blood loss the ambulance attendants had bound her wrists to stop further blood loss and started fluid replacement.

'We need blood-typing for a full blood transfusion,' Alex said as she came in answer to his call for help to stabilise the woman. He was switching a bag of fluid over, replacing an empty isotonic solution aimed at boosting the fluid levels with another. 'Then another catheter inserted. Try the anticubital fossa in her other arm first and if you can't get a 16-gauge in there so we can pump fluid in faster, you'll have to try to get one in her leg.'

Gabi found herself praying she'd have success with inserting another catheter in the girl's arm. Although she'd inserted hundreds of catheters into the femoral vein in a patient's leg, the technique, using a flexible wire to guide the needle, was slower and more likely to cause complications for the patient later.

She was lucky, and, with some blood removed and a second access open, more fluid could be fed into the patient's depleted vascular system. Once two to three litres had been infused Alex would assess the girl's response, then decide whether or not whole blood would be necessary.

'If she was in the ICU she'd have a central venous catheter inserted to monitor the venous pressure,' Alex said, looking worriedly at the girl's colourless lips.

'As soon as you feel she's OK to move again, that's where she'll go,' Gabi reminded him. 'And they've the facilities to do a cut-down far more easily and effectively up there than we have down here.'

She didn't add that although all students learnt to do 'cut-downs'—the technique of cutting into a vein in the neck or upper chest to insert a catheter for either infusion of fluids or to monitor central venous pressure—under normal circumstances they weren't encouraged to do it in A and E, where conditions made it more possible for an infection to develop in the wound.

There were also any number of complications that could ensue, including pneumothorax if the needle should puncture the lung, or internal bleeding if the cut did too much damage to the blood vessel.

Thinking of work as she checked the girl's blood pressure stopped her considering the terrible despair the youngster must have been suffering that she'd taken such drastic measures. And to have lost as much blood as she had she'd either opened her veins in the correct manner, along them rather than across them, or she'd not been found for a long time after doing it.

And I'm afraid of going up in a plane! Gabi thought, and probably shuddered because Alex touched her shoulder, as if to comfort her, though he couldn't possibly have known her thoughts.

'The second lot of fluid's working,' he said, nodding at the oxygen saturation monitor. 'Thanks.'

Gabi left the cubicle and was making her way back to the main station to find out who was next when she passed the man Alex had treated for shock earlier. He was sitting on a gurney, drinking a cup of tea.

'Feeling better?' she asked, and he nodded, but the depressed look on his face suggested that 'better' was a relative term.

'You're still worried. Did you have someone else in the car with you? Someone who was more seriously injured?'

He shook his head then said, 'No, that's wrong. I did have someone in the car. My wife. Have you been pregnant?'

The question was so unexpected it startled Gabi, then she put two and two together.

'The pregnant woman was your wife? But surely someone's told you? She's fine. Her specialist has seen her and, although he advised her to rest when she got there, he said she could go home.'

'Exactly,' the man said bitterly. 'Which, according to the nurses, is just what she did. It's why I asked if you'd been pregnant.'

Totally confused, Gabi nodded.

'Did it take over your life?' the man demanded. 'Did it consume you to the extent that no one and nothing else mattered?'

Had it? Gabi wondered.

Certainly Alex's reaction had made her draw in on herself, but...

'Your wife had a shock, and I guess her first concern was for the baby.' Even as she said them, she knew the words weren't going to offer any comfort whatsoever to this poor man.

'So was mine!' he snapped, right on cue. 'But I thought of her as well, of both of them. But did she care about me? Obviously not, or I wouldn't be sitting here on my own while she's swanned off home in a cab.'

Gabi sighed, but only inwardly. She'd seen more domestic arguments in her years of working in A and E than most people saw in a lifetime.

'You were probably still being treated. You went into shock, you know.'

'She didn't even ask about me. I asked the nurses and the woman on the desk. She doesn't care. All she cares about is the baby.'

'Dr Gabi Graham to Room Five.'

The message, repeated twice, as all pages were, reminded Gabi of the backlog of patients the accident would have caused, but she was reluctant to simply walk away from this man.

'Have you talked to her about this? Told her how you feel?'

The man laughed, but so harshly it made Gabi's skin prickle.

'Of course I have. Or I've tried to. But from her view I'm being childish and behaving badly because I'm no longer the sole focus of her attention.'

That 'focus' word had sure been getting a workout lately, Gabi thought, while another bit of her brain sought for some advice or comfort she could offer this man.

But, short of suggesting he feign a relapse and be hospitalised for further tests in order to grab his wife's attention, she couldn't think of anything, and the overworked staff, including Alana up in the admissions ward, mightn't be impressed if she suggested that option.

'You might both need some counselling. In fact, I'll see if I can get someone from Patient Services to come down and talk to you now. He or she might be able to suggest something that would help, or at least put you in touch with someone who might have some ideas.'

As her name was called again she excused herself, but paused on her way to Room Five to ask Roz to get someone down to talk to the man.

'Mr Hargreaves? Oh! I was just going to see him. His wife phoned in tears because she'd forgotten him. She'd been so concerned about the baby—'

Gabi held up her hand.

'Don't tell me, tell him,' she pleaded. Then she grinned and added, 'And lay it on thick about how upset she was. That'll do him more good than all the counsellors in the world.'

But the incident—or the ramifications of it—stayed with her. So much so it was still on her mind much later when, work finished for the day, she went up to the oncology ward to visit Jane.

Pushing open the door into the room, and seeing her ex-mother-in-law alone, she asked the question that had been bugging her since that morning.

'Did I get totally self-absorbed when I was pregnant? To the extent I shut Alex out?'

Jane's furiously wiggling eyebrows and contorted facial expressions told her it was the wrong thing to be asking, and, with the sick feeling that goes along with putting one's foot in it, Gabi turned to see Alex leaning against the wall on the far side of the room.

'Well, did I?' she demanded, asking the question of him now—not sure if it was him or herself with whom she was angry.

'Not overly so,' he said quietly, his dark eyes meeting hers but not telling her a damn thing. 'You're thinking of Mr Hargreaves? I heard he'd been talking to you.'

Gabi was about to question the 'not overly so' remark when an almost imperceptible shake of Alex's head warned her off the subject, and he stepped forward, making sure she didn't pursue it but explaining to his mother about the morning's accident.

Conversation turned to more general matters, but as they walked home together—well, it would have been stupid not to—she searched for a way to bring up the subject again and, not finding any subtle way of putting it, asked outright.

'Did you answer my question for your mother's sake— is that why you said, ''Not overly so.''?'

They'd stopped to wait for a break in the traffic so they could cross the road, and Alex turned to Gabi, his eyes searching her face as if to read some hidden subtext to the question.

Then the break came, and he took her arm and held it while they crossed.

'We were at odds with each other before you became pregnant—over going to Scotland. Then you felt it was sufficient reason for us to change our plans. I guess it was natural that I wondered if you'd done it deliberately, so that skewed my view of it—and everything that happened after it.'

He was talking so calmly it would be easy to believe that none of it had touched him deeply, but Gabi knew him well enough to guess that the words he was offering were being weighed and measured then dusted of emotion before he let them pass from his lips to her ears.

She wanted to argue over his 'our plans' statement, but that would have been petty. Besides, she remembered her own impression, when she'd lain in bed this morning, that she'd have to go a long way back—well before the pregnancy—to find their happy times.

'Can you remember where it started, the being at odds?' she asked, as she tried to remember what it had been like. 'Did it have an actual beginning or was it just niggly stuff that grew?'

Alex glanced her way and she glimpsed a slight frown before it was wiped away and he asked, 'Does it matter now?'

No, of course it doesn't, she should have said, but it would have been a lie because it did matter—at least to her.

'I suppose knowing why ours fell apart might make a difference in another relationship. Might save it foundering.'

'Have you another relationship in danger of foundering?' he asked, and Gabi realised they'd stopped walking and Alex was frowning at her, only this time it wasn't just an eyebrow twitch of a frown—this time it was the real thing, a full-blown, full-on scowl of a frown.

She turned away, moving on, climbing the steps into the apartment building.

Perhaps the 'our plans' had helped, because she'd suddenly remembered the birth of their problems. In fact, the expression on Alex's face as he'd asked about relationships had been just the same as when he'd announced that he'd made enquiries about specialising overseas, and she'd argued that, although she'd like to work overseas at some stage of her career, she didn't know that they should go right then. His mother was still grieving and needed them, and because of the length of time specialty studies took, Gabi had explained, she'd prefer it if he did them at home.

You'd have thought his shoe had bitten him, he'd been so shocked. And shocked on two counts—firstly that she hadn't automatically agreed with him, and secondly by her decision not to specialise but rather to stick with A and E, with heading that department in the children's hospital as her ultimate goal.

His reaction had made Gabi wonder if she'd lost all her identity—and, in Alex's eyes at least, had become nothing more than an extension of himself. At the time it had infuriated her so much she'd probably said some very rash things.

But no matter what she'd said, even pointing out that for him to enquire about studying overseas without discussing it with her was an indication of the way he was thinking about her position in his life, he hadn't listened. He'd shut himself off from any discussion because, in his view, no matter how she wrapped it up in reasons and excuses, she was letting her fear of flying dictate the terms of both their lives.

And though in the end she'd given in, reluctantly agreeing to go to Edinburgh with him, the argument had caused such divisions that it had only been natural it had flared again when she'd become pregnant.

And had wanted to stay in Australia until she'd had the baby.

Naturally, he'd accused her of doing it deliberately!

'I would never have done something like that!' she muttered as he followed her into the foyer, then, realising she'd spoken aloud, she turned to him to find him nodding, as if he'd followed every strand of her tortuous thought processes.

And agreed with her?

Hardly likely.

Gabi stepped into the lift and pressed the '2' button. When the lift stopped she got out, offering 'I have to see Alana' as an excuse. She did have to see Alana but, in truth, Alex's company—and probably the conversation they'd been having—was causing so much tension she needed to unwind a bit before facing him again.

Or not facing him! Though she'd have to see him briefly as she shifted her things from her flat to Alana's.

CHAPTER FIVE

'YOU'RE doing what?' Alex roared, when he caught Gab
laden with bags, trying to get out of the flat while he wa
still in the shower.

'Shifting down to Alana's.'

'Oh, for Pete's sake, Gabi, aren't you overreacting jus
a little here? Can't we behave like civilised people an
share a flat for a couple of weeks without any drama?' Hi
eyes narrowed. 'Or is it that you can't trust yourself to b
in the same flat with me?'

He was so close to the mark that Gabi had to force
scoffing laugh from her throat.

'Don't kid yourself, buster!'

She was about to explain when he turned away, stridin
across the living room then back again to hold out his arm
in a supplicating pose.

'And how do you think this is supposed to make me feel
I come back, thinking I might stay a while, and now I fine
I'm forcing you out of your own home? Are you findin
ways to torment me? Is it a punishment thing?'

'Tormenting you? Punishment? What on earth are yo
going on about?'

'That dragon, for a start,' he fumed. 'Seeing you slin
around with that animal sinuously curved around you
body. Isn't that a deliberate tease? And the hair? I com
home, you look like Gabi, then before the day is don
you've changed. Gabi's gone and some new fashion plat
is in her place.'

'Judging a book by its cover now, are you?' Gab

84

snapped. 'I'm still the same me, and I'll have you know the hair had nothing whatsoever to do with your return. And for your information you are not forcing me out of my home—and I repeat, *my* home—I'm merely doing Alana a favour. She's going away tomorrow and needs someone to mind her pets, and as all my clothes are still in carry bags it's easier for me to shift down there than to be running back and forth between the two flats.'

But she might as well have kept her mouth shut for all the good that explanation did. Alex did at least wait until she stopped talking, but the rational part of the explanation had obviously passed him by.

'And that's another thing. Why are all your clothes in carry bags? Was the flat broken into? Were all your clothes taken? Have you done something about better security since it happened?'

Gabi sighed, and dropped the bags she was still holding onto a chair.

'I need a cup of coffee,' she muttered, heading for the kitchen.

She also needed to get away, but she couldn't just walk away, leaving Alex in a welter of guilt over her departure. Neither could she admit that she *was* moving out because of him. After all, she'd fed Alana's pets before without shifting into her apartment.

But in spite of all that had happened between them—the bitterness and pain, the arguments and recrimination, the twelve months' separation—her body still responded to Alex's presence with a neediness that frightened her, while her heart, which had been well behaved for a year, now did scrunching and fluttering things whenever she caught sight of him or sensed he was near.

He'd followed her into the kitchen, so it was happening now, the uncontrollable organ pumping so wildly she suspected she was glowing pinkly all over. She was certainly hot enough to be aglow.

'I'll make the coffee,' he offered, then, stepping past her and turning to face her, he added, 'Do you have to move right now? Is Alana expecting you so soon? Couldn't we at least eat together?'

It wasn't exactly a plea, but as Alex rarely asked for anything Gabi guessed the invitation had been an effort. Coming to terms with his mother's illness must have been a strain, and he'd spent so much time with Jane over the weekend, he wouldn't have had time to contact other old friends.

Apart from Diane.

'I suppose we could,' Gabi said, then realised how grudging she'd sounded when she saw Alex's face.

Remorse struck her and she reached out and touched his arm.

'I'm sorry, I shouldn't have said it like that, but you suddenly lobbing back into my life hasn't been easy for me either.'

'Or cheap, if the number of plastic bags you're shifting to Alana's is any indication.'

Wrong thing to say! Alex realised as Gabi's eyes flashed anger as visible as lightning in a night sky.

'The clothes I bought had nothing whatsoever to do with you, Alex Graham, any more than changing my hair was prompted by your sudden return. Don't kid yourself I'd go out and get a new wardrobe to impress you. You! A man who wouldn't notice if I went to work in jungle greens or wore pyjamas out on a date.'

'I'm sure I'd notice the pyjamas,' he said, keeping his voice mild while another voice, far more strident but within him, demanded to know, if not for him, then for whom had she bought the new clothes?

Surely not for Josh Phillips, with his flashy sports car! The man's reputation with women preceded him wherever he went but he'd run a mile if things got serious. And Gabi wasn't his type. He went for obviously attractive women—

Like Gabi was now?

But Gabi wouldn't understand a man like that.

She'd be hurt.

'Possibly!' the woman he was so concerned about said dryly, and he had to think back to the original conversation to make sense of the word.

'Possibly stay to dinner?' He hazarded a guess.

'Possibly notice pyjamas,' she corrected, then she turned away, pulling packets out of the freezer, opening the pantry—getting ready to prepare their meal?

'We could go out,' he suggested. 'Down to Mickey's or somewhere else if you'd prefer.'

'Mickey's is closed on Mondays now,' she told him, her back to him as she poured rice into a colander and rinsed it under cold water. And standing there, watching her, the sense of familiarity was so acute it was as if he'd never been away.

But he *had* been away—even before he'd physically left the flat—and, remembering, he felt a sense of loss so strong it made him want to yell in protest.

'Could you open the packets and pop them in the microwave? They'll need ten minutes on defrost then another five to heat.'

He lifted the packets she'd pulled from the freezer. Thai food—one laksa and one curry—the brand name on the packets familiar.

'Hey, wasn't this the place where we used to eat back in our student days?'

Gabi nodded.

'They've started packaging their meals for freezing and the ones I've had so far have been great.'

She spoke so calmly he realised she couldn't possibly be feeling all the convoluted emotional stuff he was suffering and that knowledge added to his gloom because, in spite of all that had happened between them, he'd always harboured a dream that some day, somehow, Gabi would again be his.

The year apart had given him a better perspective of what had gone wrong between them. Though he hadn't realised it at the time, he'd taken his father's death so badly it had coloured all his thoughts and actions for the year that had followed it, so when his mother had started seeing another man he'd been angry for his father, and horrified for himself that women could be so fickle. Unable to handle his inner turmoil, he'd opted to go away, and specialising in Scotland had been about as far as he could get.

Then Gabi had protested, said she should have been consulted—behaved, in fact, in a most un-Gabi-like way. Or so he'd thought at the time.

Now, seeing the woman busy in the kitchen, he wondered if he'd ever really known her. Surely he had…

Gabi had realised as soon as she'd agreed to have dinner with him that it was a major mistake. Working near him, passing him in the corridors at A and E was one thing, but being back in a kitchen—their kitchen—with Alex was a very different matter!

For a start, she was remembering times they'd begun preparing a meal together, then ended up doing something entirely different. Often not eating until hours later—or next morning when, ravenous, they'd fed each other breakfast.

In fact, she'd always suspected their baby had been conceived one wild night in this very kitchen—a night when

vine had helped smooth the bumps they'd been experienc-
ng, and making love had reminded them of the transcen-
lent joy they'd shared.

She sighed, then felt Alex's arm brush against her shoul-
ler as they passed in the narrow space. The flash of heat
ven such an accidental touch could generate warned her
o beware. Loving Alex before had led to pain so great
he'd sometimes wondered if she'd live through it.

Loving Alex again—with the totally overwhelming pas-
ion she'd once felt for him—would surely lead to more of
he same.

Anyway, given what had happened on Saturday morning,
oving Alex now—loving anyone now—was just not an
•ption.

She poured the rice into boiling water and checked the
ime, then, as she set two plates on the divider, she knew
he couldn't continue being this close to Alex unless she
lad something to distract her.

Anything!

Conversation?

'So how was your day? Did you do any A and E work
n Scotland or go straight into an intensive care unit?'

Not a brilliant conversational gambit but better than the
ilence between them. Silence that seemed to have the abil-
ty to carry vibes from his body to hers and string webs of
nemory between them.

'I spent time in A and E, but was more called in to
onsult rather than doing shifts there. Depending on the
evel of experience of the A and E staff on duty, I'd some-
imes be called to do an IV cut-down to insert a catheter
nto an adult or an intraosseous access line into a child.
Emergency procedures rather than anything else, although
ve'd also advise on admission from time to time.'

Gabi was glad he'd answered her second question rather

than the first, because talking about his day could lead back
to the couple injured in the freeway accident, and from
there it wasn't far to things she didn't want to talk about.

Determined to keep the conversation neutral, she told
him of the child she'd treated who'd needed an intraosseous
needle inserted so fast fluid resuscitation could be given.
'It was my first go at it, and though I knew exactly what
to do—penetrate the skin and subcutaneous tissue down to
the bone, then insert the needle at a ninety-degree angle—
I was terrified.'

She glanced at Alex and shivered as the memory returned.

'It was the screwing motion to get it through the bone
that got to me. Got to the parents too. The mother was
crying and the father threw up, and I'm trying to get it in
and remove the stylet and do it all properly while not losing
my breakfast as well.'

Forks joined the plates on the divider, and she dug out
a couple of paper napkins and then left the kitchen, because
the conversation wasn't doing much to block the vibes.

She flipped through the CDs, discarding what she considered party stuff—this was definitely no party—deciding
on a Macy Gray, because she liked it, then wondering if
perhaps it was too romantic, but the moody Alanis
Morissette CDs she'd played lately weren't what she was
looking for either.

Hopefully, Alex wouldn't read anything into her choice.

Back in the kitchen, the rice was ready, the convenience
food conveniently heated and all she had to do was serve
it. Alex had slipped around to the far side of the divider
and was opening a bottle of wine.

'It's a very light white I actually bought in France the
weekend before I came back. I stuck it in my backpack

because I knew if I left it there, Angus, the guy I shared a house with, would knock it off without a second thought.'

Angus! What had this man been like? It seemed totally unbelievable to Gabi that there was an entire year of Alex's life about which she knew nothing. Together since they'd started their pre-med training, it seemed they'd always known each other. They'd met all each other's friends, then their new friends had been mutual. And now Alex had an Angus—and who knew how many other people?

Including women!

There'd have to have been women.

Had the weekend in France been a farewell to one of them?

Only on that last weekend he hadn't known he'd been coming back for good.

Or had he? Had talk of a quick visit to see his mother been a ploy to get him established in the flat?

And if so, why, for heaven's sake?

She finished serving the meal and pushed a plate across to him, nodding when he lifted the bottle of wine towards her.

Wasn't wine supposed to relax you?

Wine from France…

'The food's good,' he offered, and she realised she was staring into space, fork poised above her plate, while her mind roamed in realms she'd only read of or seen in movies or on television.

'You stuck it in your backpack,' she repeated. 'If you only brought the backpack you mustn't have intended staying. What made you change your mind?'

Dark brown eyes studied her across the table, but if she thought she was going to get an answer to her question she'd have to think again.

Alex shrugged his solid shoulders, then shook his head as if to emphasise there was no answer.

'Seeing Mum was the main reason for coming, but I did pack all my stuff back at the house and leave Angus with instructions for forwarding it if necessary, so staying must always have been an option in my mind.'

Which sounded reasonable enough to Alex, but Gabi was frowning over it, as if some flaw made it less than believable. The truth was, he wasn't sure himself what had changed his mind. Seeing his mother had been part of it. And knowing she'd not be able to travel to Scotland to see him, and that as his work grew more demanding he'd have little time to make the long trip home, had added more pressure.

But before that there'd been a sense of homecoming as the cab had driven from the airport to the apartment building, and though Gabi's behaviour had done much to shake the foundations of that feeling, something of it remained.

Something of his feelings for his ex-wife also remained, and though he told himself it was the sense of unfinished business, he wondered if it wasn't more than that. After all, there'd been other women in his life in the interim—Diane Kennedy for one wouldn't have knocked back a physical relationship had he wanted it—but none of them had appealed the way Gabi always had. None of them had stirred something deep within him.

It was probably just a physical thing. After all, there was hardly a square inch of this flat that didn't hold some sexual memory. Gabi moving into Alana's flat might at least put a damper on his less honourable urges.

He sipped his wine, hoping it might relax him, and asked about Alana's course, then about her current pets.

'Does she still have the snake?'

Gabi shuddered.

'Fortunately, no. It must have recovered enough to be set free. The only time I had to caretake while it was there it was hibernating, so I didn't have to look at it, let alone consider feeding it.'

'That terrible bird's still there,' Alex said, and Gabi found a smile.

'I know—it *is* terrible, isn't it? But only because it's about four hundred years old and has lost all its feathers. It looks worse now because it's started shredding the little vests Alana knits for it. At first she thought it might have an allergy to wool, but she's tried every available synthetic as well, and it still unravels them so its grey-blue carcass is on view to the world.'

'And what else? I saw a pouch over one of her kitchen chairs. Is she still taking in orphaned wallabies?'

'Only the very, very tiny ones,' Gabi told him. 'And Madeleine's become interested enough in the Wildlife Rescue Service to volunteer to feed them during the day.'

The doorbell rang before Gabi finished her sentence, and Alex, either because he was closer or from habit, stood up and crossed the living room to answer it.

As if conjured up by the conversation, Madeleine stood there.

'Oh, Alex, I'm so glad someone's here. Ingrid's cut herself and I can't stop the bleeding, and Graham's never at home when he's needed.'

'Grab our first-aid kit, Gabi,' Alex responded, taking control as if he'd never been away, assuming she'd still have the carefully stocked kit he'd put together when they'd first moved in together.

Then, no doubt knowing Gabi would follow, he hustled Madeleine across the foyer towards the stairs. Walking up to the Frosts' flat would take less time than summoning the lift.

Gabi hauled the hefty case out of the hall cupboard and followed, arriving in time to see the beautiful Swede clutching Alex's shoulder, and to hear his next order.

'Phone an ambulance, Gabi. I could suture it here, but it's deep and best done under sterile conditions.'

'It'd be quicker if I drove her over to Royal Westside,' Gabi pointed out, but Alex shook his head.

'We need to keep her leg elevated, and we can't do that without a stretcher.'

He was applying pressure to a towel held high up on Ingrid's inner thigh, and as Gabi dialled the emergency number and waited for a response, she wondered how such an accident could have happened.

And whether Ingrid *had* to lean quite that close to the man administering first aid!

Ignoring the unworthy thoughts—she no longer had any right to be jealous where Alex was concerned—Gabi gave the necessary instructions to the emergency control room and hung up. Alex must have been watching her, for she'd no sooner released the receiver than he was giving more orders.

'Roll a bandage into a pressure pad and we'll tie that onto her leg.'

Gabi opened the first-aid case and found a square of material which she obediently fashioned into a solid pad, but it wasn't until Alex removed the towel to put the pad in place, and blood spurted out, that Gabi realised why he'd insisted on an ambulance. His talk of stitching under sterile conditions had been to calm Ingrid, and possibly Madeleine—though she was somewhere else in the flat, no doubt calming the twins. Ingrid's wound had gone deep, rupturing a blood vessel, which would need microsurgery for an effective repair.

As the pad quickly reddened with escaping blood, Alex

cursed and used his hand once again to clamp the damaged vessel more tightly closed.

'I'll go down and wait for the ambulance,' Gabi offered, when she was satisfied there was nothing more she could do to help Alex, who'd need to hold his hand where it was until they reached the hospital. 'I suggested they drive into the basement car park and I'll need to open the doors.'

The ambulance arrived far sooner than she'd expected and, knowing there'd be enough people to squash around the stretcher in the lift, she directed them to the fifth floor and stayed in the basement.

But Alex was the only one accompanying Ingrid when the lift doors slid open on the return trip. Accompanying and comforting if the way she was clinging to his free hand was any indication.

Gabi quelled the urge to demand that the woman unhand her husband—after all, it would sound unnecessarily dramatic, and on top of that she was reasonably sure he was no longer her husband. She'd signed papers ages ago, but hadn't read the reams of accompanying instructions so hadn't a clue what happened next as far as divorces were concerned.

'Did you hear me?'

Alex's cross demand made her flinch—he was still a grouch after all!

'No, I didn't, as it happens,' she snapped right back. 'What orders are you issuing now?'

He frowned at her, then shook his head as if her behaviour was beyond his understanding.

'Madeleine wondered if you'd sit with the twins for a while. I'll go in the ambulance with Ingrid and walk back when they take her to Theatre, but Madeleine feels she should be there while they operate, so she knows exactly what's happening and can let Ingrid's parents know.'

Gabi sighed but didn't bother answering, merely walking into the still open lift and pressing the button for the fifth floor.

Would Alex have accompanied Ingrid to the hospital if she'd been overweight, worn glasses and had a face like a horse? Especially when an ambulance attendant could have applied pressure to the wound?

Probably, honesty forced her to concede.

But you wouldn't be feeling so unsettled by his actions, now, would you? Gabi demanded of herself. So now who's a grouch?

Up on the fifth floor the identical twin boys were bathed, pyjama-clad and ready for bed. With their blond hair and shining blue eyes, they gave the impression of being a couple of angels, just dropped down to earth from a soft fluffy cloud. But Gabi knew better. She'd helped out with the holy terrors before. Though tonight they were both sitting in front of the television, watching quietly, so maybe they'd improved.

Madeleine explained the nightly routine—really tough stuff: a story, then bed—and was about to leave when Gabi knew she had to ask.

'How did Ingrid cut herself so badly in such an awkward place?'

Madeleine shrugged.

'Working in A and E, you probably see more stupid accidents than most, but I'd think this one beats them all. She was carving a pumpkin. She spent a year as a nanny in the United States and now has the idea of spreading Hallowe'en far and wide throughout Australia.'

'As if we don't have enough commercialised holidays!' Gabi groaned. 'Though it's already begun out here. I know of kids going trick-or-treating, though I don't know about the pumpkins.'

'Well, we won't have a pumpkin—I threw it away,' Madeleine said, then she showed Gabi the list of phone numbers she'd left. Both her own and Graham's mobiles were on it, as well as the hospital number, in case it had slipped Gabi's mind.

Assuring the agitated woman she'd manage, Gabi almost thrust her out the door.

Which was when the twins gave up the angel act and reverted to their normal devilish selves. First Shaun—or was it Ewan?—pushed Ewan—or was it Shaun?—off his little chair, and within minutes it was full-scale war. Gabi was attempting to negotiate a peace deal and wondering if the UN had people who could help when the phone rang. Knowing she'd not hear a word, she lifted the closest twin, tucked him under her arm and threatened the other with immediate banishment to bed if he so much as breathed. Then she grabbed the receiver and muttered a grating hello.

'Is everything all right?' Alex's voice sounded anxiously in her ear. 'You sound a little stressed.'

'I am not a *little* stressed. I am enormously stressed,' Gabi informed him. 'I just hope it wasn't your idea that I mind the twins, because if I find it was you'll be looking for alternative accommodation.'

Alex chuckled, the sound bringing far too much warmth in its wake.

Damn the man, even over the phone he could affect her.

'Did you want something in particular?' Gabi muttered, as the twin under her arm began to drum his heels against her legs and the other began to cry for Ingrid.

'Madeleine asked me to check you were OK. Will I tell her yes?'

'If lying through your teeth sits well with you, then yes,' Gabi told him. 'Otherwise you can relay the message that both are still alive, though if the one under my arm doesn't stop kicking this may only be temporary.'

Alex chuckled again, then assured her he'd be there to help just as soon as he could.

'I'll go by the flat and bring up our meals. We can reheat them in the microwave. You're probably crabby because you haven't eaten.'

It was fortunate he hung up so quickly as her reply to that remark wasn't at all ladylike. Though the idea of food was good. She'd just tie the kids to their beds first!

Much to her surprise, physical restraint proved unnecessary. Once in bed, the pair resumed their angel guise, and as she read about Bob the Builder and his friends all working to repair a road, they both drifted off to sleep, leaving Gabi to finish the story on her own.

Just to see how it ended.

She was still sitting in their bedroom, in a chair between the two little beds, when the doorbell rang. She reached out and brushed her hand over the soft cheek of the little boy nearest to her, and wondered what life might have been like now if her child had lived.

CHAPTER SIX

ALEX raised his eyebrows at the silence in the house.

'Did you gag them as well as tie them to their beds?'

Gabi grinned at him.

'No need to do either. They reverted to their angel act and went quietly off to sleep while I was reading the story.'

She felt Alex's eyes studying her face and hoped he wouldn't read the remnants of the longing the sleeping children had reawoken in her.

Apparently not, for he carried the tray on which he'd put their dinner plates, the glasses and the bottle of wine through to the kitchen and, after studying the microwave for a moment, set it to heating first one plate of food, then the other.

But as they sat, at a table this time, to finish their meal, Gabi realised his ability to read her mood hadn't been diminished by a year apart.

'I lost that baby too,' he said, touching his glass to hers in a silent salute. 'I know I'd been unhappy over the timing of it, but it was still my child as well.'

Gabi put her glass down on the table, afraid her fingers might lose the ability to hold it, in the same way as her lungs had lost their ability to breathe. And the air trapped in her chest was causing pain behind her sternum.

In the end, she nodded and, as her body slowly resumed normal duties, even managed to speak.

'I suppose I did know that, but I shut you out, didn't I? I told myself you hadn't wanted the baby so couldn't possibly have felt the same way. In a way, I guess I almost blamed you, though that was an emotional reaction, Alex, not a rational one.'

He smiled, but with a sadness that added heartache to the trouble in Gabi's chest.

'I can understand that, because I felt the same way, felt guilt because I hadn't wanted a baby—not right then,' he said quietly. 'At the time you were flat out, coping with your own emotions, and I wasn't much help there, so why should you have helped me, or even reached out for me? Though maybe if we could have mourned together it would have helped us both...'

'Instead of finally splitting us apart,' Gabi finished for him. 'So many maybes,' she added, as something of the closeness they'd shared for so long wrapped around her like an old, familiar blanket.

An old, familiar blanket full of holes, her head scoffed, while her ever-hopeful heart was banging away in her chest, as if this mild rapport and understanding meant something.

Which it doesn't, Gabi told it, trying desperately to think of a less personal topic of conversation. It was the shock of seeing Alex again that was causing the physical and emotional reactions. She was a doctor, and she knew shock did funny things to people, so she'd be a fool to read too much into them.

'I'm doing the rescue training course at the weekend.' The new topic had come to her in a flash and, grateful for any conversational crumb, she'd leapt on it before considering the consequences.

'*You're* doing the rescue training course?'

'You don't have to sound so incredulous!' she grumbled. 'A "Good on you, Gabi" would have been a far better reaction.'

'But you'll have to abseil over a cliff. You hate heights.

And it's only for people who intend to volunteer for the rescue chopper. You won't do that.'

It was his certainty that infuriated Gabi. She pushed her plate away and rose to her feet, jammed her fists onto her hips and glared at him as she said, 'Oh, won't I, now? Well, that just shows how little you know me, Alex Graham. Because I'm not only doing the course, I've also been added to the chopper's roster so, providing I pass this weekend, I could be doing rescues within a fortnight.'

She doubted whether he'd have looked more surprised— shocked, flabbergasted, take your pick—if she'd turned into a green and purple striped alien on the spot.

Still infuriated, she swiped her empty plate off the table, took it into the kitchen, where she washed and dried both it and the fork, then dumped them on the tray ready to take back to her flat.

Alex watched her storm away. Watched the way her body moved as if to a tune only she could hear. It was so familiar his body stirred in response, yet he was becoming less and less certain that he really knew this woman. Which, in its own way, was even more physically tantalising!

But setting sex aside—and what was new in that—he needed to figure out what had caused the changes. Something must have triggered a sudden decision to not only change her looks and her entire wardrobe but to take such positive steps to overcome her phobia of heights.

Heaven knew he'd tried to help her over it often enough. When they'd first shifted into the apartment building it had been weeks before she'd ventured near the door leading onto the balcony, and, from the dismal look of the plants out there, she still had trouble walking further than the door.

Why did people change?

Because they were dissatisfied with their old selves?

Maybe over a period of time that would be true, but all at once?

'Hello-o? Earth to Alex! I've asked you three times if you want a cup of coffee.'

He hadn't even seen her come back to the table, but she was definitely there, leaning towards him so he couldn't help but notice the way her breasts pushed against the splashy flower on her T-shirt.

It had to be a man. Nothing else could explain such extreme changes of image and of self all at once.

Josh Phillips!

'Yes, thank you,' he said, pleased the words sounded civilised enough, even though they'd been forced out through clenched teeth.

Maybe it wasn't Josh Phillips. If Gabi was determined to get over her fear of heights and flying, maybe it was an airline pilot.

But where would Gabi meet an airline pilot?

He realised he had no idea—not just about where she'd meet an airline pilot, but where she'd been going and what she'd been doing for the past twelve months. In his mind, she'd been wrapped in a time warp—living in the flat, going to work and returning home, and in her free time keeping in touch, as Gabi always did, with both her family and his.

He watched her progress as she carried two cups of coffee over to the table, and once again the familiar-unfamiliar dichotomy struck him.

But doing the rescue training course—that was so far beyond unfamiliar he still couldn't comprehend it.

Or was the instructor the attraction? Not an airline pilot but a helicopter pilot? The rescue pilots led the training

ourses because they needed to know the capabilities of all
ne medical staff they took on board.

'I'm off this weekend. I could come with you, do the
ourse—be there for you.'

'Be there for me, or be there to laugh when I faint from
error at the top of the cliff?'

She was stirring the sugar in her coffee, watching the
poon swirl the dark liquid round and round, as if the action
equired all her concentration.

'So you acknowledge that's a likely scenario?'

She looked up, her gold-flecked hazel eyes meeting his
earlessly.

'Of course it's a likely scenario. But once I've recovered
ne cliff will still be there, and I'll still have to go down it
f I want to go on to the next stage of the training. So, if
ou want a good laugh, by all means, come along.'

Couldn't be the helicopter pilot. She'd hardly have
vanted the new love interest meeting the old.

Hell! Was that really what he was? Gabi's old love in-
erest?

'I think I'll watch some television.' She was carrying her
offee into the living room, her comment interrupting his
nner debate. 'Now the kids are asleep there's no need for
ou to stay. You can probably scowl just as easily down
n my flat as up here.'

He knew his scowl deepened—couldn't stop it—but she
vas right, he'd be better off somewhere else. Maybe some-
vhere else he'd stop being so obsessed with the changes
e couldn't help but notice. Even little things like now,
vhen she had more or less ordered him to go.

Contrariness made him want to stay, but then he remem-
•ered what Gabi had been doing before they'd started their
nterrupted dinner. She'd been shifting her gear down to
Alana's. Because Alana was going away. Tomorrow!

But if anyone knew what was happening in Gabi's lif
it would be Alana, and wasn't this the ideal opportunity t
ask her? He'd carry some of Gabi's stuff down to Alana'
flat and bring up the conversation very casually.

'I will go,' he said. Then, as Gabi turned a bemused loo
on him, he realised there must have been a long gap be
tween her suggestion and his response. So he added, 'No
I've finished my coffee,' so it didn't sound as if he'd com
pletely lost his mind.

Bringing up the subject of the change in Gabi conversa
tionally didn't work, so in the end he asked Alana outrigh

'What's got into Gabi with all these changes?'

Alana shrugged her slim, elegant shoulders.

'Beats me, but it's about time.' She studied Alex for
couple of seconds then added, 'I thought at first it migl
be your return but she assured me it wasn't anything to d
with you, and it's not like Gabi to lie about something lik
that. She mightn't answer, but she'd cut her tongue ou
rather than tell an outright lie.'

Alex's moody slouch around Alana's living room ha
brought him up against the parrot's cage, and he lifted
corner of the night-blanket and peered at the unattractiv
bird.

'I'd have said she'd cut her tongue out—or a leg off—
before she abseiled down a cliff, but she tells me she'
doing that on Saturday.'

'She's doing what?' Alana shrieked. 'Gabi? I don't be
lieve you.'

'Believe me!' Alex said glumly, though he was please
Alana's reaction mirrored his own.

'Well, the change thing only started on Saturday,' Alan
told him, after she'd done a bit of pacing herself. 'Mayb
someone died in A and E—someone our age—and it jolte

er. It mightn't have been specifically Friday night—it
could have been any night that week—but because she was
working nights all week she couldn't put her plans into
action until the weekend.'

'I guess!' Alex said, and although he definitely regretted
the death of anyone as young as he considered he, Gabi
and Alana to be, he infinitely preferred that option to a new
man in Gabi's life. 'Though she's seen plenty of young
people die in A and E over the years.'

'And plenty younger than us,' Alana agreed, but she
didn't seem inclined to throw any further light on the matter, or to offer him coffee, so he said goodbye and went
back to the fourth floor where he sat at Gabi's desk and,
mindful of her privacy, only looked at the top layer of
papers strewn across it.

There wasn't a note saying 'Met a great new man' anywhere that he could see! And by now he was feeling thoroughly ashamed of himself as well as confused. He found
a clean piece of paper and wrote Gabi a note explaining
he'd taken her clothes down to Alana's, put it on the chair
where the bags had been and went to bed. Maybe the remnants of jet-lag were making things so confusing.

Gabi returned to find the note. It was late and she was
tired—lack of sleep over the weekend catching up with
her—so she phoned Alana and promised she'd be down for
orders first thing in the morning, then showered in her own
bathroom and went to bed.

But tonight an awareness of Alex in the flat, and the
memory of Alex, scowling at his coffee, made sleep impossible. She thought back to what he'd said, about mourn-
ing their baby, and regret as thick as dust clogged her
throat.

If only, as he'd said, they'd been able to share the pain—

to grieve together and offer comfort to each other. Wouldn't that have healed the breach?

Or was it only hindsight that made such things seem possible?

And now?

She turned onto her back and stared at the ceiling, silently acknowledging the dark shadow lurking behind all that was bright and new in her life.

Now it was good that she and Alex were estranged, because if, like the lotto, her number came up in the draw for HIV, she could cope with it on her own, without the pity and distress she knew it would cause those she loved—and would have caused Alex if they'd still been married.

If they'd still been married she wouldn't have been able—or willing—to hide the incident and its attendant risks from him, so their estrangement was a plus.

And if her heart still leapt when she heard his voice, and her body still heated whenever he was near, and her lips still hungered for his so-familiar kisses, that was for her alone to know, because now was not the time to be getting involved in a relationship—with *anyone*!

Except perhaps a four-hundred-year-old featherless parrot!

'Ouch!' Gabi withdrew her finger from the parrot's cage and sucked it. 'And to think I finally fell asleep determined to like you!' she told it.

'You don't have to like him, just feed him,' Alana reminded her, bustling into the living room with a list that looked like a small book. 'Madeleine's taking the joey,' she said, waving her hand to where a makeshift pouch hung over a chair. 'So you can ignore the instructions on feeding it. The guinea-pig nuts are in the brown tin and the cat food's in the blue one. I put an extra bowl of cat food on the balcony—will you be all right on the balcony? There's a stray somewhere in the neighbourhood and I'm worried it's not getting enough to eat.'

Gabi took the notes, assured Alana she'd manage, then kissed her friend goodbye. But before she could move away Alana caught her arm and drew her back, looking into Gabi's eyes as she asked, 'Are you OK? Is something bothering you? Do you want to talk about it?'

'What is this? Last-minute guilt about leaving me to feed your brood? Don't I look OK?'

Alana's gaze skimmed over her, taking in the green shirt and white skirt that had been Gabi's favourite purchase the previous Saturday.

'You look more than OK. You look brilliant,' Alana admitted, 'but Alex said something about the rescue training course. *You* abseiling down a cliff?'

Gabi grinned at her.

'I'm changing my life,' she said, 'but hopefully not my friends. Not unless they start questioning what I'm doing and nagging at me for reasons.'

'Hey, *I* don't nag,' Alana reminded her. 'I'm your original "live and let live" girl.'

Gabi hugged her.

'I know you are. Have a great time in Melbourne, send a postcard and I'll see you when you get back.'

She paused and frowned at her friend.

'Which is when, by the way? Have you ever said? Is it on the list?'

She waved the papers at Alana, who was smiling with excitement.

'Three weeks—isn't it wonderful? Three whole weeks away from the stresses of Ward Eight B.'

Gabi knew her answering smile wasn't quite good enough, though she managed to stay cheerful while she said goodbye, but by the time she reached the lift she was muttering to herself about people who deliberately didn't mention the length of time when asking, casually, if you'd take care of their pets.

You wanted to get out of your flat, she reminded herself, but the reminder didn't soothe her agitation. If anything, it made her feel even crabbier.

The lift failed to arrive, so she took the stairs to the ground floor, hoping to walk off her mood. But if it had happened to improve with the exercise, it blackened again when she emerged into the foyer to see Alex standing there—holding the lift door open—with Kirsten clinging to his arm, both of them laughing like hyenas!

'Oh, Gabi, fancy preferring the company of Alana's awful strays to this gorgeous man's. I got my heel caught in the lift and, look, like the Prince in *Cinderella*, he not only rescued my shoe but insisted on putting it back on.'

Gabi forced a smile to her lips, though inwardly acknowledged that while she could probably—just—cope with the knowledge that Alex was no longer hers, there was no way she could handle him being someone else's— not if that someone else was a friend and she'd have to see them together.

Laughing!

She fell in behind them, surprised Kirsten could walk so smoothly in the spike-heeled shoes, infuriated because Alex seemed to be fitting his stride to hers, something he'd rarely remembered to do for Gabi in all the years they'd walked to work together.

Thinking spiteful thoughts will give you wrinkles. She reminded herself of her mother's adage, repeated since Gabi's childhood.

But it was hard not to think spiteful thoughts when the

wo of them were chattering and chuckling as if they were
ld friends, while she, Gabi, was the outsider.

'Come on, slowcoach,' Kirsten called back to her when
ne pair stopped before crossing the road. And once again
Gabi had to force a smile, only this time she had to swallow
ne bitter gall of jealousy as well. She added a second or
wo to her pace, coming abreast of them as the traffic
leared. And Alex took her arm as well as Kirsten's, hur-
ying them both across then stepping back so it was he who
walked behind.

'He's gorgeous,' Kirsten whispered.

He's mine! Gabi wanted to shout, but he wasn't any
nore and that was that.

'You're judging by looks again,' she said instead, re-
ninding Kirsten of her disastrous habit of falling for hand-
ome men.

'Not entirely,' Kirsten said with great dignity.

'No! I forgot!' Gabi muttered. 'You rode down in the
ift together—a trip as long as a lifetime.'

'Hey! Don't get miffed with me!' Kirsten told her in a
whisper that was probably still loud enough to reach Alex.
If you're still interested, just say so. You know I'd never
oach another woman's man. But you did shift down to
Alana's. I thought you couldn't bear to be near him. And
ou've never, in all the time I've lived near you, talked
bout him, so I kind of assumed your relationship really
was dead and buried.'

So did I, Gabi thought—until he came back.

But she couldn't admit this to Kirsten so she apologised
or snapping and agreed to meet in the canteen at one, if
Kirsten was free from her occupational therapy duties and
Gabi herself could also get away. With this arranged, she
eaded for A and E where, hopefully, she'd be so busy

she'd have no time to think about all the confusing things happening in her life right now.

At least that wish came true. It was after seven in the evening before Gabi finally felt justified in leaving the department. The day had begun with a group of pre-school children brought in after a gas leak near their kindergarten had triggered not only a full-scale emergency in the inner city suburb but a lot of breathing difficulties.

Not to mention hysteria on the part of the majority of parents who'd been alerted by the news flashed from radio and television newsrooms and who, in some cases, had beaten the ambulances to the hospital.

Now, following Nat Bell, the young intern from her team, into the tearoom, she collapsed into a chair.

'I don't think I've got the energy to go home,' she moaned, kicking off her shoes and leaning forward to massage her toes.

'I'll drive you,' he said eagerly. 'It's not out of my way and if you like we could stop for something to eat so you don't have to cook.'

Gabi smiled at him, knowing the offer was one of kindness rather than interest.

'She can't be going out to dinner when the parrot and cats and guinea pigs are starving,' a deeper voice said, and Gabi turned to see Alex, like herself, collapsed in another chair.

He grinned at her in surprise, then added, 'Great day wasn't it?'

'I can't believe those parents behaving the way they did,' Nat said. 'Some of them were far worse than the children and seeing their mother or father hysterical made the kids worse.'

'I liked the little girl who bit her mother. Did you hear about it?' Gabi included Alex in the conversation. 'I was at the stage of biting the woman myself, she was going on so much, when the little one—she couldn't have been any older than the twins—sank her teeth into a perfectly manicured finger.'

Alex chuckled and moved his chair to sit in front of Gabi as Nat added, 'And I don't think it was the first time it had happened, because the woman shut up immediately.'

'Lie back and relax.' This from Alex, but the suggestion was so sensible Gabi didn't argue, though the last thing she'd expected was for Alex to pick up her feet and take over the toe massage she'd been giving herself.

'It's OK,' he said to Nat, who was watching this liberty with a frown. 'When Gabi and I were married I did this all the time. I know just how she likes it.'

Was it the suggestiveness in his voice or the ecstasy of his fingers pressing deep into the soles of her feet that sent heat ricocheting through Gabi's body? She should sit up, retrieve her appendages and get right away from the man, but it was so good...so relaxing...so very, very sensual...only a masochist would have moved, or ordered him to stop.

And only an idiot would let it go on.

The idiot won.

In the end she was so relaxed she had to force herself to stay awake.

'I've got to go,' she said, reluctantly removing her feet from Alex's magic touch. 'If I don't go home right now I'll fall asleep in this chair, and Alana's birds and animals will start e-mailing her to come home because she's left them with a feeding failure.'

She struggled to her feet, surprised to see by the time—eight-fifteen—that she must already have been asleep.

'Have you been here all the time?' she demanded of

Alex, when she realised they were the only two left in the room.

'I was watching over you,' he said with a teasing grin. 'You still sleep like the dead. That poor young man on your team was talking to you for at least five minutes before he realised you were out of it.'

'That poor young man?' Gabi queried, as she followed Alex out the door into the cool night air. 'What makes you sorry for him?'

'I'm sorry for anyone suffering the pangs of unrequited love. Fellow feeling and all that.'

'There was nothing unrequited about our love,' Gabi reminded him, 'so don't pull that pathetic act on me. There might be lots of reasons why our marriage didn't last, but me not loving you was never one of them.'

They were walking along the footpath into patches of light thrown by streetlamps then dark shadows before the next light illuminated the scene, so when Alex stopped and, by the simple expedient of grasping her elbow, stopped her as well, she turned to him but couldn't see his expression.

'And now?' he demanded, his voice as hoarse as if he'd been running to catch up with her. 'Can you say that now? Can you say not loving me will stop us getting together?'

'You can't ask me that,' Gabi said, the pain in her chest rendering the words as breathless as his had been. 'There's been no talk of getting back together! We're divorced— aren't we? And you came back to see your mother, not me.'

'Ah, but did I, or was I just looking for an excuse?' he murmured, then he eased his head down towards hers and brushed his lips across her mouth—a silent question this time.

Gabi felt the fire that oh, so-light contact caused, and

panic took over from all other emotions. She'd checked on HIV infection before she'd left the hospital on Saturday morning. What had the latest info said?

Apart from the point five per cent, there were transmission details. Use a condom, but you can't get HIV from normal social contact, or from dancing together, or from kissing.

Kissing was OK?

She closed her eyes and saw the printed words she'd read, confirming her desperate recollection. Then she sighed and pressed her lips to his, realising how quickly all the jostling thoughts must have raced through her head because Alex's lips had remained in place, awaiting the answer she was now offering.

You know where kissing leads, her head reminded her, but kissing Alex was like coming home after a long and weary journey, so she kept on doing it.

She'd think about the consequences tomorrow.

The blaring of a car horn, followed by raucous cheers and yells of 'Go for it' from the car's passengers, woke her up to the fact that she was standing on the footpath of a very busy road, kissing her ex-husband.

'I've got to get home to feed the animals!' she muttered as she broke away from him.

Alex made no comment, simply falling in beside her, and because she was striding out—hurrying away from what had happened?—he *did* match his pace to hers.

They reached the building and its well-lit foyer and she glanced towards him, wondering if she'd read any reaction to the kiss in his face.

It told her nothing. Typical! He might be able to read her like a TV guide, but when had she ever been able to read what Alex was thinking or feeling?

'If you like, I can fix us something to eat while you do

your duties at Alana's, then you could come up and have dinner in your own home.'

Gabi looked properly this time—taking his face feature by feature—but still failed to come up with any clue as to what might be behind this invitation.

More kissing?

Uh-uh!

'I don't think so,' she said, and, deciding she too could do the mysterious thing, she didn't elaborate.

Not that the refusal fazed Alex. He simply nodded, then said, 'OK. In that case, I might walk back and visit Mum. Goodnight.'

And with that he was gone. No goodbye kiss, no nothing.

'You didn't want a goodnight kiss,' Gabi reminded herself as the lift arrived and she stepped in.

'No?'

The question startled her, then she saw who'd asked it and chuckled.

'No!' she said firmly, acknowledging Daisy's presence with a smile. 'Though if I keep talking to myself I might need to see you professionally. Do you offer advice and counselling to adults—about adults, I mean—or do you only do children? And can I come or would I have to phone in to your talk-back show or visit your website?'

The lift had stopped on the second floor and as Daisy stepped out Gabi remembered she, too, had to get out.

'I'm staying at Alana's. Minding the pets,' she explained.

'And keeping out of your ex-husband's way?' Daisy guessed.

'That too,' Gabi acknowledged, at the same time wondering for the umpteenth time how information filtered its way into Daisy's flat. The woman rarely appeared in daylight hours, she barely socialised, and after a year in the building no one really knew her.

Yet every time Gabi did see her Daisy seemed to know exactly what was going on in her life.

And everyone else's.

'Is it osmosis?' she asked, when she realised Daisy was still in the foyer, fumbling through a great bunch of keys to find the one to open her door.

Daisy turned, eyebrows raised, and Gabi explained.

'That you always seem to know everything.'

Daisy laughed.

'I know you all think I'm a hermit, but I do get around, you know. But because I kind of fade into the background, people talk about all kinds of things in front of me.'

'Maybe you should have been a psychic or a medium, instead of a psychologist,' Gabi suggested. 'You'd know all the questions as well as the answers.'

'I doubt anyone knows them all, Gabi,' Daisy said, and, finding the right key, she unlocked her door, said goodnight and disappeared—still the mystery woman of the building.

Gabi, following Alana's instructions, fed and watered the menagerie, carefully noting down on a calendar above the fish tank that she'd fed the fish. No need to do them for another couple of days—she'd killed off Alana's fish in the past through over-zealous feeding.

By the time she finished the cleaning part of the routine it was after ten and, not wanting the bother of cooking, she pulled a couple of slices of frozen bread out of a packet in the freezer, dropped them into the toaster and with a packet of soup mix from the pantry made herself a cup of soup.

Soup and toast. What would Alex have cooked?

Alex?

Much as she didn't want to think about him she knew the kiss had shifted the goal posts of their present relationship.

What present relationship?

Exactly! She had to think about it.

There *is* no relationship, she told the voices in her head. It died back with the baby, if not before that.

CHAPTER SEVEN

IT SEEMED the rest of the week was determined to follow the pattern set on the Monday, and busy days followed busy days. So by Friday Gabi was regretting her decision to do the rescue course. Though, on the other hand, maybe being thoroughly exhausted would lessen her fear.

After refusing—see point number six on her list—to accompany Kirsten out raging on Friday night, she went to bed early, but that didn't stop her cursing the alarm when it went off at six on Saturday morning. Grumpy with tiredness, she forced down a bowl of cereal, then realised she'd probably be bringing it up again in the not too distant future.

'Great!' she muttered to herself, walking down the stairs to the basement in the hope the exercise might make her feel better. She was in baggily stretched jeans and an old T-shirt that had been in the laundry basket last weekend and had thus escaped the fate of the rest of her old clothes. Though the clothes felt familiar and comfortable, they did nothing to stop the butterflies doing sambas with the cereal flakes in her stomach.

'Oh, no! I don't believe it. Didn't I tell you I didn't need any onlookers on this exercise? Why aren't you in bed? You've had as busy a week as I have, so why not sleep in today? You've already done this rescue course so you could only be coming along to laugh at me. Well, if you think I'm giving you a lift, think again.'

Alex straightened up from where he'd been leaning against her car, but that was his only reaction to her furious outburst. Until she got closer, still grumbling under her breath, and he plucked the keys from her fingers and unlocked the car.

'It's an hour's drive to Mount McConran, so you can have another hour's sleep on the way. In you get.'

He'd kind of herded her towards the passenger door and was now holding it open.

She gave him a look she hoped held enough fury for even someone as insensitive as Alex to get the message, but as her preferred alternative, knocking him out with a punch to the jaw, probably wasn't realistic, or even possible, she climbed into the passenger side of the car.

'Don't think I'm giving in,' she told him, when he slid into the driver's seat. 'I'm just too tired to argue with you right now.'

'I realise that,' he said, his face as deadpan as ever as he started the engine and reversed out of her parking space. 'And I'll be only too pleased to let you yell at me later.'

She thought about kicking him, but that might cause an accident, and it would also mean lifting her leg, and right now both of them were still heavy with sleep—and it was so nice to be driven for a change that she might just close her eyes for a few minutes.

Alex revelled in the feeling of being behind the wheel of a car again, though he'd have preferred something with more power than Gabi's baby VW, especially as the long haul up the mountain began. He glanced her way, wondering how on earth she was going to handle being at a cliff edge, let alone abseiling down it. No matter that the cliffs they started on were small, and the instructors had them double-harnessed to make sure there'd be no accidents. Gabi's fear lay in the nothingness beyond the level ground.

But though his gut knotted at the thought of her terror, he knew nothing would persuade her not to do it once she'd set her mind on it. Which brought him back to why? Why would a woman so terrified of heights decide, after five years working in A and E, that she wanted to be part of the rescue-team roster? After talking to Alana, he'd intended checking back through the previous week's A and E reports to see if perhaps a young woman *had* died, giving Gabi a jolt about her own mortality.

At thirty?

He shook his head, admitting to himself that nothing made any sense, and going over and over it wasn't helping. And he wouldn't think about kissing Gabi either as mental arguments about that—why he'd done it, why she'd responded, whether that achingly familiar, fiery response meant anything—had kept him awake most of the previous night.

The road narrowed, and the car was enveloped in a green gloom. He'd reached the high land, where tropical rainforest nurtured the land with leaf mould, and the thick, lush growth crowded close to the car as if threatening to reclaim the road.

Was it the coolness or a sense of a journey almost completed that woke Gabi? She sat up suddenly, and looked around.

'I remember coming here when you did your course,' she said, sounding almost surprised that the memory had lingered. 'I know I chickened out and went nowhere near the cliff edge, but I always thought we should come back some time, perhaps spend a weekend in the mountains.'

'We still could,' Alex suggested quietly, slowing down so he could turn to see her reaction to his words.

But the shift of emotions was too swift for him to analyse, though he was sure he'd seen excitement before wariness and then a sadness so deep it caused a hitch in his breathing.

'We're not a "we" any more, Alex,' she reminded him, then turned her head and stared out at the wild jungle, isolating him as effectively as a cattle dog cutting a beast from a herd.

Gabi saw the vine-entwined palms, the broad-leafed ferns and vivid green of moss-encrusted rocks, but her brain processed none of these things, too busy trying to calm a heart in double jeopardy—with Alex and the task ahead of her.

Then, as suddenly as if someone had turned on a light, they left the cool darkness of the forest for a field of green, and ahead of them a parking and picnic area, built to take advantage of a spectacular view. Able to admire such beauty from a distance, Gabi stared at the wide sweep of land spread before them.

'Great, isn't it?' Alex said, and she agreed, though now they were pulling into the parking area and she could see the small group of doctors and nurses clustered around a man in a safety harness.

The butterflies in her stomach, dormant while she'd slept on the journey up, resumed their activity, though now it was more a wild Scottish reel than a samba.

'It's a big group,' Alex remarked.

'Change of rotation for the interns next week. I've never worked out when and how the nurses change jobs but I know the younger ones in A and E seem to be constantly on the move. So much so I never learn the names of some of them. Not so I could call them by name with any certainty.'

And how someone about to make a total fool of herself can chatter on about nurses' names, I don't know, Gabi's head voice muttered at her, but chattering on about anything was better than cringing in her seat and making little

whimpering noises, which was what she'd really have preferred to be doing.

Alex pulled up alongside an ambulance.

'Well, at least they're prepared for me,' Gabi told him,
determined not to let the whimpering coward loose. Not
yet, anyway.

She climbed out of the car and, without waiting for
Alex—any delay might weaken her resolve—marched over
to where the group were now putting on harnesses. By concentrating on the people, and when necessary looking else-
where on the far horizon, she could avoid thinking about
the fact that twenty metres in front of her the ground
dropped away into nothingness.

'Dr Graham by two,' the man who was obviously the
leader said, then he looked beyond her at Alex. 'Hey, man,
you're back. I thought the department must be breeding
Grahams when I saw two more names on my list. How was
Scotland, and what are you doing here? Bigwigs like you
don't usually do rescues.'

Alex strode past Gabi and shook the man's hand.

'I'm not a bigwig yet, Pete. I'm still in training and
thought I'd better update my Superman skills in case
they're ever needed.'

He must have sensed Gabi trying to edge away from
behind him, for he reached out, caught her arm and drew
her gently forward.

'This is Gabi. She's terrified of heights but for some
reason has decided on a kill-or-cure approach to her fear.
Treat her gently, will you?'

Light blue eyes, the faded colour of the sky on a hot
summer day, skimmed over Gabi, then a reassuring smile
warmed the man's rugged face.

'I'm Pete,' he said, holding out his hand. 'I guess we

should let you go first so you don't have all the agony of waiting.'

He kept the hand she'd offered him and led her forward, talking all the time about the harness and how it worked and how, in a rescue, she wouldn't be abseiling but would be lowered, so perhaps for the first time she might like to try that experience.

'We'll let you down slowly, so it's just like going down in a lift. All you have to do is try to land on your feet rather than in an inert heap on top of the imaginary patient.'

'I should be able to manage that,' Gabi told him, though her teeth were practically chattering with fear and her knees were showing an alarming tendency to wobble. She just hoped he couldn't hear the voice that was yelling, No, no, no! in her head.

Pete talked all the time as she buckled on her harness, as he led her to a section of the cliff where an overhang made the lowering process much easier, and as another member of the rescue squad abseiled down before her.

'He'll be waiting at the bottom for you,' Pete told Gabi, attaching a rope to her harness. 'Now, do you want to look down to see where you're going, or just do it?'

Gabi looked frantically around, searching for Alex, for anyone or anything familiar, but she couldn't see him among the crowd laughing and joking as they buckled on their harnesses and tested the ropes on which they'd swing over the cliff. Not that he'd have been much help, she told herself.

'What's best?' she asked Pete, when the decision proved too much for her.

'I think it's best to look, so you know where you're going, but if it's going to freak you out so much you're a blubbering mass of jelly then don't look.'

Not wanting to be seen as a blubbering mass of jelly,

he opted not to look, simply obeying instructions and moving towards the edge of the cliff, listening all the time to Pete's instructions while reciting over and over to herself, I can do this, I can do this.

And she did, sitting first on the edge of the overhang—looking out, not down—then turning and lowering herself until she felt the harness take her weight.

'On the chopper, once you're confident the harness is always there and always able to take your weight, you'll sit and go out forwards,' Pete explained, 'but here you'll feel better if you can see the cliff in front of you.'

Did she feel better, she wondered, as the cliff face slid past her eyes? And better than what? Bloody terrified?

But she wasn't panicking, and that was good, and she'd resisted the temptation to look down, which was even better, as looking down would have undoubtedly brought a hysterical reaction not good when dangling on a rope.

'Got you,' a voice said, and strong hands grasped her waist and guided her feet to solid ground. The voice had sounded so like Alex's she looked not down but around, to see who had caught her.

'How did you get here? It wasn't you who abseiled down,' she said, when his grinning face confirmed her suspicions.

The grin grew even broader.

'It was, you know. I even said I'd see you at the bottom, but you were so scared witless I doubt you'd have noticed a meteorite landing next to you or heard a brass band playing.'

'I didn't—I wasn't—I...' Triumph at her achievement was vying with the disturbing elements of being held by Alex, so the things she wanted to say died *en route*. Marshalling all her brain power, she tried again.

'Shouldn't I be getting out of this gear?'

Alex's hand caught hers as she tried to unclip the rope.

'Not yet. You've got to go back up.'

'I've got to go back up?' she quavered.

'How else are you going to get back to the top?'

Gabi looked around and realised, for the first time, just how narrow a ledge her landing place was. Alex was standing between her and the edge, so she hadn't considered there might not be solid ground beyond him. Panic seized her by the throat and her body grew rigid with fear.

'Don't let it get to you now,' he said, once more following her thoughts. 'You're hooked up and I'm hooked up, and as soon as I give a couple of tugs on your rope Pete will have you lifted back to the top in no time.'

Gabi was just assimilating this information—with only a modicum of the panic lessening—and reminding herself it was what she was determined to do, when Alex added, 'And then you can abseil down the other side. Listen to the rest of them yahooing. It's great fun!'

The 'fun' suggestion was so stupid she didn't dignify it with an answer, though she did raise her eyebrow. The rest of what Alex had said sounded vaguely familiar—no doubt because Pete had said the same to her earlier. So, to prove she wasn't scared quite as witless as Alex presumed, she gave the necessary tugs on her rope and allowed herself to be lifted back to the top of the cliff.

It was the beginning of countless ascents and descents, all small triumphs in their own way, but by early afternoon, though the butterflies had been banished—or were at least under control—Gabi's legs were so tired she knew she'd be foolish to keep going.

'I love crew who know when to stop,' Pete said, when she explained she'd had enough, 'because I don't want dead heroes on my missions. But you'll be back tomorrow?'

Gabi assured him she'd be there. Tomorrow, as well as

doing more abseiling and lowering practice, they'd be looking at the equipment the helicopters carried, and learning to put together the lightweight backboards and braces and how to strap them on to accident victims while teetering on cliff edges or dangling in space.

'You realise you'd rarely be called upon to go over the edge of cliffs?' Alex said as he drove them back down the mountain.

Gabi nodded. Unless a patient was so severely injured he needed stabilising before being moved, the regular rescue team would bring him either up to the helicopter, if it was a chopper rescue, or to more secure ground in a cliff rescue, where the medical personnel would then take over.

She stretched her calves and rolled her shoulders, thinking of the bliss of a warm bath, too tired to feel any triumph about conquering the baby cliffs she'd swung out over today. Although it *had* been a triumph, particularly at the end when she'd been able to look down to where she was going without total pandemonium breaking out in her stomach.

'Why are you doing it?'

Alex's question brought her out of her self-congratulatory mood.

'It was time,' she said flatly, remembering some of the silly reasons—flying to Europe to see *Alex*; she must have been off her head—she'd given herself when she'd written it on the list.

He gave her a look that suggested he didn't believe her, but said nothing, so she let the silence settle around them and looked out at the passing scenery, so different now the light was fading, casting the world in softer, more mellow colours.

She must have slept again—was it an escape mechanism—because the next thing she knew they were in the basement of the apartment block and Alex had switched off the engine.

The car, small at the best of times, seemed to shrink around them so the air was charged with both their life forces competing for the space.

'You must know all the stuff Pete does tomorrow,' Gabi said, as the strange vibes made her skin fidget.

'I won't be going. I've missed seeing Mum today, and by the time I've showered and grabbed a bite to eat it will be too late for visiting hours, so I'll spend more time with her tomorrow.'

Gabi knew she should feel relief, which some parts of her undoubtedly did, but she also felt a twinge of disappointment and, given her current situation, even small twinges of disappointment, connected to Alex, were *not good*. Best she get out of the car.

'You'd better give me my keys,' she said, as he automatically slipped them into his pocket on their way to the lift.

He passed them over as the lift doors opened, and she felt his fingers brush against hers, igniting the electricity that still sparked between them.

She clenched the keys so tightly the sharp edges dug into her palm, but that pain was better than giving in to electricity—sparky or otherwise.

Once safe inside Alana's flat she reviewed her options. Option, really. There was only one, and that was to avoid Alex at all times, at all costs. The phone rang as she was telling the revolting bird about it to reinforce her decision, and when Alex's voice asked if she'd like to have dinner with him, she panicked and said, 'No, I'm sorry. I'm going out.'

She hung up before he could lecture her on the need to get a good night's sleep and phoned Kirsten, who'd already invited her to a party at a friend's place. Now she'd have to go, so her response to Alex wouldn't be a lie.

The throaty roar of an engine brought Alex out of a deep sleep. It took him a few minutes to work out where he was and get the present sorted from the dream. Then, wanting a glass of water before he went back to sleep, he got up and walked through to the living room on his way to the kitchen. Curiosity took him across to the sliding glass doors, where he peered out over the balcony to see if he could work out what had woken him.

The little sports car he'd seen outside the hospital was parked opposite the entrance to the units. Empty.

Had its arrival woken him, or had it been parked there for some time? He turned away to get the glass of water.

It's none of your business what Gabi does, or with whom, he reminded himself, but anger knotted his intestines and soured the water he was drinking. It drove him to the phone but, though he lifted the receiver, sanity returned before he had time to dial Alana's number and he sank back onto the bed and tried to work out where and how things had gone so wrong between himself and the woman he still loved.

Not that thinking about it helped. And talking about it to his mother next morning failed to throw any light on the subject. Though she did say one thing that he carried home with him, mulling over it as he shopped then carted the groceries back to the flat.

'If you want her, woo her.' Simple enough words, but they'd stuck in his head. His mother's contention was he'd done it once, so surely he could do it again. Pretend Gabi was someone new he'd just met and go from there.

By the time he'd put away the groceries and, feeling extremely virtuous, vacuumed and tidied the flat, he'd decided it was the way to go. He'd start tonight. In fact, he could go down and tape a note on Alana's door, asking Gabi to phone him when she got in. Then he'd suggest dinner.

She'd said no to dinner last night!

'That's because she had a date with Josh.'

Saying the words aloud added more force to them, and reinforced his doubts about the wooing-and-winning strategy.

Flowers. He'd often bought her flowers when they'd been courting. Perhaps if he taped the note *and* a flower on her door. Where would he get a flower?

He peered out the window and saw the sports car back, right in front of the entrance. The man part of Alex wondered how the devil Josh always got a parking spot right in front of the building, while the would-be lover felt fury build.

He would *not* give in.

He'd forget the flower and go down right now. She must be home if Josh was here.

Rather than wait for the lift he took the stairs, erupting out of the fire door on two and charging towards Alana's flat. A relatively polite ring of the bell brought no response, and as his over-active imagination supplied him with any number of unwanted scenarios being played out behind the door, he stuck his finger on the bell and kept it there.

'I think she's just gone out again,' a quiet voice said, and he spun around to see the door to the second flat open, and a woman with pale green eyes and a cloud of black hair peering anxiously out at him.

And frowning.

'I know you, don't I?' she said, and Alex, thinking back, remembered the woman moving into the flat opposite Alana's not long before he'd left.

'I'm Alex Graham,' he said, removing his finger from the bell and crossing to offer his hand.

Her slim fingers were cool and he felt that coolness calming him. He peered behind her, trying to remember what he knew of her—whether she was married, had children, kept pets as Alana did—but his mind was blank.

'Daisy Rutherford,' she said. 'We did meet, not long before you went to Scotland. Would you like to come in? Do you want to wait for Gabi? I'm sure, after the big day she's had, she won't be long.'

Alex found himself ushered into the flat, even accepting a beer when it was offered. The frustration he'd been feeling—after all, how else should a man feel when he'd taken the big decision to woo and win back his wife then found she wasn't there to be wooed or won—slowly drained away as Daisy's quiet voice asked him about Scotland and the year he'd spent there.

He remembered she was a psychologist who worked—where? Not at the hospital. Somewhere strange.

But, wherever she worked, she was undoubtedly good for he was feeling far more relaxed.

Though a spike of resentment remained lodged within him and in the end he had to stand up and oh-so-casually wander across to her glass doors, which overlooked the street in front. The sports car was gone, confirming his suspicions, and suddenly even Daisy's gentle conversation wasn't enough to calm him.

He finished his beer, thanked her for her kindness, then left, taking the stairs back to the fourth floor two at a time—the spike driving him on. He cooked himself a steak and slapped it between two slices of bread. Bachelor dinner! Then watched television until he fell asleep in front of it, waking at two with a stiff neck and what felt like a dislocated hip.

But that didn't stop him rising early, dressing with more than his usual attention to work clothes, then hanging around in the foyer of the building, trying to look as if he wasn't waiting for someone.

'Gabi's gone,' Kirsten informed him, tripping out of the lift with a warm smile on her face and a cloud of perfume enveloping her slim form. 'Do you like this?'

She moved closer.

'It's a new perfume I'm trying. I've always gone for flower scents before, but I was reading in yesterday's paper that men are usually more attracted to spice and musk in a woman's perfume. I knew Alana used that kind of thing, so I went down earlier to borrow some and caught Gabi as she was leaving.'

Kirsten had taken his arm and was guiding him out of the building as if they walked arm in arm to work every day. But she did it so naturally, and her manner was so unaffected, he could understand why she and Gabi had become friends.

'Well?' she demanded.

He turned towards her, not understanding, and she sighed.

'I might just as well be invisible as far as you're concerned, mightn't I? I was asking about perfume. You're a man, you see, and it's like flowers having nectar to attract bees—women wear perfume to attract men. But if it's not the right kind, I won't buy it.'

Alex sniffed the air. Actually, he'd been breathing in the perfume since she'd exited the lift so his nose had got used to it. But now he concentrated, and pronounced it very nice.

'You'd probably say that about it if I was wearing vanilla, or gin, or something else out of the kitchen.'

'Definitely the gin,' he told her. 'Or sesame oil—that's got a great smell.'

'On a woman?' Kirsten's screech was so disbelieving he laughed and she looked at him, then said, 'Yes, I can see why Gabi fell for you.'

He wanted to press for more information—like how she knew how Gabi had felt and if she was privy to Gabi's feelings now—but they were at the hospital, and other workers were greeting both of them.

'Have a good day,' Kirsten said, when they parted in the lobby outside A and E. Then she waved her wrist in front of his nose. 'And think about the perfume. I'd like something more than that very weak ''nice'' you offered earlier. Actually, I could do a test on you—try out a few to see if the article was right. Will you be home tonight? Or any night this week? I could offer you dinner.'

She was so pleasant he couldn't say no, or tell her he intended using whatever wiles he had at his disposal to tempt Gabi out to dinner tonight, and if that worked every night for a week—or two—or maybe a year. He made an indeterminate kind of noise and walked on into the department. Not seeing Gabi anywhere, he approached Roz Cooper at the desk.

'Is Gabi around?' he asked, and she, too, looked around. 'She was here a minute ago. We were watching you sniff Kirsten's wrist, and she was saying she thought only dogs sought out partners on the basis of their olfactory sense.'

'Ouch!' Alex said, while a sinking feeling in his stomach suggested that wooing and winning his wife might not be as easy as his mother had made it sound.

CHAPTER EIGHT

GABI focussed on her patient, an elderly woman, Mrs Elsie Armstrong, sent to the hospital by her GP when a regular blood test had showed an alarming decrease in her haemoglobin count. As a consequence of this, the woman was breathing heavily as her body battled to get enough oxygen to her brain.

'Can you tell me what medication you're on?' Gabi asked, and blue eyes, still bright though greyed by age, gave her a scornful look.

'Of course I can. Everyone should know what they're taking and why.'

'Good!' Gabi told her. 'Then fire away.'

And fire away the patient did, though, even with the oxygen she'd been given when she'd first come in, she had to pause from time to time to catch her breath. She knew her drugs right down to the dosages: ninety milligrams of Adalat, a drug to reduce blood pressure, thirty milligrams of Lasix, a diuretic to prevent fluid retention, and one Zantac, a ranitidine hydrochloride drug designed to prevent recurrence of a duodenal ulcer but which could also be used as a preventative for reflux.

And if the woman had had problems like that once before, then a bleeding ulcer, or even bleeding polyps in her stomach or intestine, could be causing blood loss and the consequent lowering of her haemoglobin count now.

'How long have you been on the Zantac?' Gabi asked.

Mrs Armstrong frowned at her.

'Ages. It seems like for ever, in fact. I had some prob-

ems in my stomach. Had to swallow one of those nasty
amera things and the specialist found some little things
hat were bleeding.'

'Polyps?'

The frown changed to a smile.

'That's what they were. He burnt them off I think, but I
ertainly didn't feel it.'

'Well, it may be that they need burning off again,' Gabi
old her. 'I think you should be admitted, so the specialists
an do some tests.'

'I didn't have to stay in last time,' Mrs Armstrong ar-
ued. 'If I stay in, who'll get Alf his tea? And what about
y toothbrush and nighties and things? I've got a hospital
ag all packed, because that's sensible when you get older,
nd it's somewhere to put the nice nighties my daughter
ives me every Christmas, but I didn't bring it with me
ecause I wasn't going to the hospital. I was going to the
octor's.'

The flow of words stopped momentarily, then Mrs
Armstrong sat up on the examination couch and added with
n air of triumph, 'Anyway, I can't stay. The car's on a
arking meter and it'll expire soon.'

Gabi checked the date of birth she'd seen on the file. If
er calculations were correct, Mrs Armstrong was eighty-
ine.

'The car's a problem,' she agreed. 'But because the low
lood count could have any number of causes, you'd be
etter off in hospital where we can run a series of tests.
nd with your haemoglobin so low you must be feeling
red. Your GP suggested a blood transfusion, and that will
ertainly pick you up while we work out what's wrong.'

She paused, wondering if the woman was listening or
gnoring her.

'Perhaps you could drive home, arrange for someone to

give Alf his dinner—we could organise meals on wheels
for him if he can't cope on his own—'

Mrs Armstrong gave a shout of laughter.

'Meals on wheels don't come for cats,' she said, chor
tling merrily at the ridiculous idea.

Gabi regrouped.

'Maybe a neighbour?'

'I guess the young woman next door might do it,' Mr
Armstrong conceded. 'After all, it's only a matter of check
ing he's got clean water and a bowl of dried food. He's go
a cat door so he can go in and out of the house.'

'Do you feel up to driving home, arranging things, ther
coming back? Do you have any way of getting back o
would you like me to organise an ambulance pick-up?'

'An ambulance driving up my street? To my house? No
thank you. I'd have all the neighbours gossiping for weeks
I'll get a bus.'

Gabi hesitated. Much as she admired the woman's in
dependent spirit, she didn't like the idea of her coming bacl
to the hospital on a bus. For a start, the bus stopped a
couple of hundred metres down the road, and the clim
from the stop to the hospital entrance would be hard fo
anyone with a depleted oxygen supply.

'There's no one who'd drive you?' she asked.

'I've got my daughter and two daughters-in-law, but
wouldn't ask them,' Mrs Armstrong said. 'They're all very
good to me, and one of my sons does my lawn, but th
girls all work and they'd have to take time off.'

Gabi's mental calculation put 'the girls' somewhere i
the region of sixty, but she gave up arguing.

'Look,' she said, 'there's an organisation with voluntee
drivers. I'll see if I can get one of them to pick you up. D
you mind waiting until I find out?'

Mrs Armstrong glanced at her watch.

'I'm on a two-hour meter and I've only got ten minutes eft.'

Gabi had to smile.

'I'll be quick,' she promised, leaving the cubicle and enlisting Roz's help in contacting the transport people.

'They'll do it, but they can't get anyone to pick you up until two,' she told her patient minutes later. 'When they drop you off, come into A and E and ask whoever's on the desk if you can see me. If you want to phone your family, you'll be going into Ward Eight B to begin with, and after the doctors there have done tests you might be transferred to another ward—one the gastroenterologist visits every day. But that wouldn't be for a few days.'

Mrs Armstrong departed, but thoughts of her lingered in Gabi's head. There was a fearlessness about the older woman that suggested she'd never been afraid of heights, or planes, or anything man or God had put on earth.

Including infectious diseases!

'Gabi, there's a little boy in Four—could you take him?'

Something in Roz's voice suggested she'd been keeping this patient for Gabi, but then most of the permanent staff knew of Gabi's interest in children and directed them her way.

She read the information already collected as she made her way to the small consulting room.

Michael McKenna. His date of birth put him at four—a much easier age to work out than eighty-nine—but as soon as Gabi met him she realised he shared the same fearlessness as Mrs Armstrong.

'There's nothing wrong with me,' he said, shooting his harassed-looking mother a fierce glare, then meeting Gabi's eyes with defiance.

'He's just not well,' Mrs McKenna said softly. 'I know I might be fussing, but he hasn't been himself lately.'

Gabi knelt so she was on a level with the child.

'Even if there's nothing wrong, your mum will feel better if I can tell her that. But I can't tell her unless I check you out. Do you hurt anywhere?'

Michael shook his head, setting dark curls bouncing around his pale face.

'You said your leg hurt, that's why you didn't want to play outside over the weekend,' his mother reminded him and got another glare for her trouble.

'It doesn't hurt now,' Michael told Gabi.

'Good,' she said. 'Now, see this, see where the numbers are? I'm going to put this just a little way into your ear and the numbers that come up will tell me if you're running a temperature. That's usually a sign that someone's a bit sick.'

Michael submitted, but only on condition he could see the numbers when she'd finished.

By then they were friends—or as close as she was likely to get in a quick consultation—so he allowed himself to be lifted onto the examination table where Gabi could listen to his chest—and he to hers—and take his blood pressure. They had a slight argument over the cuff pump, but in the end Gabi pronounced herself satisfied.

'I'd like to do a blood test,' she said to Mrs McKenna. 'The most likely diagnosis is a mild virus of some kind, but a blood test would show up anything more serious.'

The woman nodded, though the thought of anything more serious had her looking grim.

'Now, I need to take some of your blood,' Gabi explained to Michael. She found a rather tattered bear, one of many kept in A and E to use as guinea pigs, and showed on the bear what she'd do.

'See how still he sits although the needle pricks through his skin? Can you sit as still as that?'

Michael not only claimed he could, but he was as good as his word and sat watching in fascination as his blood filled the syringe.

'Do you have a local GP? I can have the results sent through to him.'

Mrs McKenna shook her head.

'We've just shifted from down south. My parents retired up here and we moved to be closer to them, but we've been busy with settling in and getting school and pre-school organised for the kids, and doctors were the last thing on our minds.'

'Well, if you phone the hospital tomorrow at about this time and ask for Pathology. Give them this number...' she wrote Michael's patient number in clear figures on a card, '...and they'll tell you the results. I'll let them know you'll be ringing.'

She hesitated, knowing she could make an outpatient appointment for Michael but not wanting to drag the child and his mother back to the hospital unnecessarily. Hopefully, it was just a virus, but that nebulous 'not well' description parents often gave could be symptomatic of so many things.

After bidding Michael and his mother farewell, she moved on to her next patient—a worker with a gashed hand that required suturing.

'I'll give you a tetanus shot as well,' she told the bulky man.

His look of horror suggested she might have to use the bear to reassure him, but after her experience over the weekend she was sensitive to fears and phobias of any kind, so she teased him into submission, pointing out he'd already had one injection when she'd put a local anaesthetic into his hand before stitching it.

'I didn't notice that one,' he admitted, and as she kept

him talking, discussing—of all things—his passion for
growing orchids, she slid the needle into his well-muscled
arm. He didn't notice that either.

'I think it's the variety I like about A and E,' she said
later, when she and the young nurse who'd worked with
her most of the morning stopped for a quick cup of coffee.
'Not only in the injuries and complaints but in the people
I know you don't get to follow through on cases, but you
get a different kind of satisfaction.'

The nurse shook her head.

'Not for me,' she said. 'To me, it's like first aid. I want
to end up on a ward and see people getting better. Or help
them cope if they're not going to get better. I like that
patient contact thing you can build up.'

'But can you these days,' Gabi queried, 'when so many
stays are short term? Even most chemo is done on an outpatient basis these days.'

The nurse shook her head.

'But three days in hospital must seem like a long time
to a patient and, outside visiting hours, the nurse is the
person closest to him or her.'

They were still arguing over it in a desultory fashion
when Alex and another member of his team walked in.
Gabi's heart reacted in what was now a predictable manner
and she had to remind herself of her determination to keep
out of his way.

Which meant finishing her coffee, putting down her cup
and standing up.

The nurse joined her, whispering to Gabi as they left the
tearoom, 'Is it true you were once married to him?'

Though she should have expected it—after all, hospitals
were notorious hotbeds of gossip—the question still struck
deep.

'Yes,' she said, when she realised the young woman was

vaiting for an answer. She'd have liked to add, Do you
vant to make something of it? But she knew such aggres-
ion would be duly reported and repeated and she'd be
eeding the very machinery she hated.

Unfortunately, the nurse was still by her side when they
assed the desk where a huge arrangement of flowers, long-
asting Australian natives like waratahs and Geraldton wax
nd kangaroo paw, was standing.

'Someone's popular,' she said to the clerk behind the
lesk. He glanced up at her and smiled.

'Seems so,' he said. 'They're for you.'

'For me?'

Duh! How could she have sounded so naïve? And with
he nurse standing there as well!

'Is it your birthday?' the nurse asked, and Gabi, recov-
ring slightly, muttered something that the nurse and clerk
ould both have taken as a yes, before seizing the arrange-
nent and heading back towards the tearoom.

They must be from a grateful patient, she decided, then
egretted not offering this explanation to her eager audi-
nce. But at the door of the tearoom she stopped dead. Alex
vas probably still in there, and walking in with an armful
f flowers might call for some explanations.

Not that it was any of his business.

But she detoured to the washrooms anyway, pushing
pen the door and plonking the arrangement down on the
ong bench that held the washbasins so she could find a
ard and see who was embarrassing her at work.

The card was small, and fitted so snugly into its mini-
nvelope that she had trouble dragging it out.

And even then it wasn't much help. 'I mean,' Gabi mut-
ered to herself, 'what can one possibly glean from "Dinner
onight" and a question mark? Who on earth might want
o have dinner with me and how do I say yes or no?'

She turned the card over, but there was no explanatory note or phone number. The young intern—his name kept escaping her, she must be going senile—had moved on with the new rotation. Would he want to dine with a senile thirty-year-old anyway? And did he imagine that now he wasn't working with her he'd have a better chance of getting her to agree to go out with him?

She frowned at the flowers, and in the end decided they were too nice to hide away, so she obeyed the instruction to give them a drink, picked them up and marched back into A and E where she put them on the desk for all to see.

Roz, back behind the desk, raised her eyebrows but said nothing, while Alex, walking past shortly afterwards, glanced her way but didn't comment.

'So you see,' Gabi said to Jane some hours later, when she'd finished work and had popped up to see her favourite patient, 'I've no idea who wants me to have dinner with him. Or maybe it's a her.'

She knew she was avoiding going home, as presumably whoever had asked her out to dinner would phone for a reply. And if it wasn't Alex she didn't want to go and if it was Alex, though there was no earthly reason why it should be, she really couldn't go.

'A her? The Queen of England?' Jane suggested.

'No, a him—the US President,' Gabi countered, and they both vied with each other to offer ridiculous suggestions until laughter made it impossible to speak.

As Alex walked in it struck him that he'd never seen his mother laugh the way she did with Gabi. If he'd been a female, would he and she—or she and she as it would have been—have laughed the same way, or was it part of Gabi's uniqueness that she could make his mother laugh?

'You're frowning. Has something upset you?'

His mother broke off first, asking the question, and from

the startled glance Gabi flung his way she hadn't expected him to be calling in at this time.

He gave his mother a reassuring smile and quite liked the feeling that he'd had *some* effect on Gabi. After all, the flowers, which were now decorating his mother's bedside table, had met with nothing but silence.

'I was thinking how things might have been if I'd been a girl.'

Now his mother was frowning.

'If you'd been a girl?' she said faintly, and because it sounded so bizarre he tried again.

'If you'd had a daughter, not a son. What our relationship would have been like.'

The frown faded and she shook her head.

'Just as good as yours and mine. Different, I suppose, in that I think women talk to each other more.' She grinned at him. 'Why? Were you thinking of a sex change? Is this something we should discuss?'

'As if!' he muttered, embarrassed his mother could even talk about such a thing—and in front of Gabi, who looked suspiciously as if she was laughing.

And why hadn't she mentioned the flowers? Said yes or no to his invitation?

'Well?' he said to Gabi, as his aggravation with what now seemed like a female conspiracy grew.

'Well, should you have a sex change? Why ask me?'

He scowled at her.

'You know very well that's not what I mean. I meant, well, what about dinner?'

'Are you asking if I'm going to eat it some time this evening? Yes,' she said, though there was no longer the light of laughter in her eyes. She glanced from him to the flowers, then back to him again. 'Did *you* send them?'

She sounded so disbelieving the aggravation swelled into righteous indignation.

'Why wouldn't it have been me? Were you expecting flowers from someone else? Josh Phillips, perhaps? But surely he'd sign a card with love and probably a ''J'' rather than an ''A''.'

Gabi stared at him as if he was mad, then slowly withdrew a tiny card out of her pocket and passed it to him.

He read it and shook his head.

'They didn't put the A. I told them A.'

He passed the card back but didn't like the look in Gabi's eyes.

'Whether they put the A or not isn't really the point, is it, Alex?'

Then she stood up, kissed his mother goodbye and left the room.

'Well, so much for your bright idea!' he fumed at his mother, but she took no notice, merely staring at the door through which Gabi had departed.

'There's something wrong with Gabi,' she said. 'I thought at first it was to do with you coming back, but that wouldn't make her so—so brittle somehow. Then late yesterday, when she was here, I felt she was distracted.'

Yesterday? Gabi had been visiting his mother yesterday—not out with Josh Phillips? His heart leapt, but before he could analyse that reaction his mother was speaking again.

'I suppose it *could* be you coming back. The timing's spot on, and if I'm right in thinking she's never stopped loving you, I suppose your sudden return could have thrown her into a spin.'

'If she's never stopped loving me, she's got a mighty funny way of showing it,' Alex growled, but he knew his mother was right. Brittle was exactly the word he'd use about Gabi at the moment. 'Damn it all, we can't keep guessing about this. I'm going to go and see her, have it out with her, find out what's going on in that stubborn head of hers.'

'Good luck,' his mother said, and it wasn't until he was nearly home he realised there'd been a wealth of irony in the way she'd said it.

But having anything out with Gabi proved impossible. There was no response to his ring at Alana's doorbell and though, when he reached the fourth floor, there were 'company' sounds coming from Kirsten's flat, he didn't feel he could knock on the door to ask if Gabi was there.

Though he could knock to tell Kirsten he'd give her perfume trials a go.

No! He dismissed the idea as soon as it surfaced. At the moment he was every bit the grouch his mother often called him, and testing perfume might push his limited supply of patience too far.

Especially if Gabi *wasn't* there, and he had to worry about where she was—and with whom!

But after another restless night Alex knew he had to resolve things with Gabi, one way or another. So, determined not to miss her again, he got up, showered and dressed, then went downstairs, only realising just how early it was when, after a long delay, a sleep-tousled figure, clutching the dragon robe around her body, appeared in the doorway.

'Alex? Is something wrong? Oh, no, is it Jane?'

She clutched his forearm, and looked so pale he put his free arm around her shoulders.

'No, she's fine—well, you saw her yourself last night.'

The feel of Gabi's soft warm body tucked against his was so right he was having trouble thinking of anything else.

'I'm sorry if I frightened you but, Gabi, we need to talk.

Or maybe you don't need to talk, but I do. I need to know things from you.'

She turned and was looking up at him, one of the golden sunny streaks of hair falling across her face, so it seemed natural for him to push it back and tuck it behind her ear, then just as natural to bend forward and brush a kiss across her soft, pale, unpainted lips.

The surge of desire as their lips met was so unexpected he could no more have stopped kissing her than he could have stopped a runaway train. And the kiss was so familiar, so obviously a prelude to love-making, he found himself tucking her closer, one hand feeding into the golden hair so he could hold her head captive, the other hand pressing her yielding body into his rapidly firming one.

She met his kiss with the passion that even after so many years of knowing her had never ceased to surprise him, a passion so at odds with her quiet demeanour and gentle nature he'd always found it mind-blowingly exciting.

His hands shifted, roving inside the dragon robe, feeling the naked skin beneath it, cool to his touch—as cool as her kisses were hot. He heard the familiar murmur as his fingers brushed her nipples and understood why none of the women he'd dated since they'd separated had ever turned him on.

It was because they hadn't been Gabi. They hadn't been that intoxicating mix of demureness and sexuality, and they hadn't made funny noises in their throats when he'd touched them. The robe was fully open now, so his hands could move at will, and with a feeling that he was reclaiming part of himself that had been missing for a long time he used touch to relearn her contours, his hearing to relearn her responses.

His excitement built until he knew it could have only

one end, but too much had happened for him to take anything for granted.

'Gabi?'

He breathed her name, knowing it was a question but
also a confirmation that she was his and wanting him as
badly as he wanted her.

She heard it—heard her name—echoing down through
some long tunnel in her mind, the word a plea.

And even through the hot red haze of desire, through the
wanting that sent an ache into every cell in her body, she
remembered the risk—the inherent danger—and pushed
herself away. It wasn't the HIV so much as the danger of
falling back under the spell of Alex's sexuality without any
of the issues that had caused their split being resolved.

Sex for the sake of it—for physical gratification.

'No, Alex,' she said, because she had to say the word,
to let him hear the negative response so at odds with her
positive reaction. 'No and no and no.'

He stepped back, flinching as if she'd struck him hard
with every repetition, then shook his head in disbelief.

'You mean it, don't you?' he demanded, his breath coming in quick shallow gasps.

She nodded, unable to speak for the lump of agonising
emotion that had risen in her throat.

'Why?' he demanded. 'And don't tell me you don't still
feel something for me, because after that performance you
must—or you've become a nymphomaniac while I was
gone.'

His harshness was like a whip lashing at her skin and
she shrank away.

'You're on your way to work, and I've got to get dressed.
Please, go.'

She straightened as she said it, determined not to let him
see her pain, though she doubted whether he'd see anything

through the scarlet mists of fury he was undoubtedly feeling.

But he did leave, and Gabi shut the door behind him, then leaned against it until her legs stopped shaking.

Was she being silly? She really needed to think this through, but how could she think when all she'd ever felt for Alex had returned a thousandfold?

If Saturday morning had never happened, how happy she'd have been to have him back—not right away, but now they'd talked about the baby, now he'd admitted how he'd felt, and when they'd talked some more about other things, and sorted out what had gone wrong the first time.

But would he have come back if his mother hadn't been ill? Didn't she need to consider that as well?

And Saturday morning *had* happened. So there was the 'protecting Alex' issue to be resolved as well. Sure, she could tell him what had happened, but then there'd have been two of them with the tiny niggling doubt squirming deep inside them, so while he'd be worrying about her she'd be worrying about him worrying about her, as well as worrying about herself.

As far as a physical relationship was concerned, he'd be upset for her but insist she was being stupid about not having one—insist the chances of her having HIV were so minimal the chances of him catching it were non-existent. He'd remind her they could use protection, but that wasn't the point. In her heart of hearts she knew she couldn't put Alex at *any* risk, no matter how infinitesimal, so a relationship with him right now was just not possible.

But how to make that clear without revealing the real reason?

Gabi groaned and slid down until she was sitting on the floor, but sitting didn't help her think any better, and the bird was calling to be let out from under his blanket, and no doubt the guinea pigs needed fresh paper in their box. And apple? Was apple on the menu for today or had that been yesterday?

But Alana's household tasks weren't enough to stop her thoughts straying again and again to Alex.

'I'm back to needing another man,' she told the bird, but doubted she had the will to find one. Although tonight was the first night of the dancing lessons she was taking. Perhaps she'd meet someone there.

'You're going where?' Kirsten demanded, as they both exited the lift a little later.

'To Latin-American dancing lessons,' Gabi repeated.

'Oh, what fun! Why didn't you tell me? I'll come too,' Kirsten announced. 'Oh, blow! I can't tonight. I saw Alex when I was jogging and he's coming to nose-test my perfumes tonight. I asked him to dinner first.'

She cast a sidelong glance at Gabi but, though Gabi knew exactly what it meant, she refused to react in any way. Actually, good luck to Alex if he found consolation with someone else. At least then he'd be safe.

That bit of her mind was lying, of course. She hated the idea of him with anyone else, and wanted to scratch Kirsten's eyes out because she'd be spending time with him.

By the time she reached work she was thoroughly confused, but all confusion was banished when she phoned Pathology in response to a message on her pager.

'The blood you sent us yesterday. Michael McKenna. Can you contact the family and arrange for them to come in? There's a query leukaemia in the test, and we'll need to do a bone-marrow a.s.a.p.'

Gabi agreed to contact them, then, knowing Josh would be the specialist in charge of the case, she had him paged. To her surprise, he appeared in person.

'I heard it was you who wanted me, so I had to come,' he said, beaming at Gabi at precisely the moment Alex walked past. 'It's about the child you saw yesterday,' Josh continued, drawing Gabi away from the desk so they could speak privately. 'I'd like to admit Michael tomorrow, but I hate people just arriving at the hospital without prior warning of what to expect. I don't suppose you mentioned leukaemia yesterday?'

Gabi shook her head, mentally consigned her debut at the dancing lessons to the following week and concentrated as Josh continued, 'No, of course you wouldn't have. Could we go to them to tell them? Where do they live? I'd like us both to go because you've met them and I can answer questions.'

'I've only met Mrs McKenna,' Gabi told him, 'and specialists don't generally do house calls.'

'I've a gut feeling about this one,' Josh confessed, 'and, as well as that, once the specific type of leukaemia is confirmed by the bone-marrow test, there's a new drug I'd like to try on Michael.'

He smiled at Gabi.

'I think I'll have more chance of getting their permission if they start off liking and trusting me.'

'I'll get the address,' Gabi said, 'although the moment I phone them and make arrangements to come they'll know something's wrong. My only instruction to Mrs McKenna was to phone the lab for the results.'

'Can you leave phoning until it's as late as possible?' Josh asked. 'I'll tell the lab to say he's anaemic, which is true, and that someone will be in touch about an appointment for further treatment.'

Gabi agreed, and went to find the file, returning to find Josh gone.

'Dr Phillips asked if you could let his secretary know where and when,' the clerk told her. 'He'll fit in with you.'

Going straight from work would be easiest, Gabi decided, and phoned Josh's secretary to tell her she'd be ready to leave at six. If it didn't suit the McKennas she'd leave another message later.

By the time her shift finished Gabi was so tired she regretted agreeing to accompany Josh, though she'd have been just as tired going dancing. Then she considered the little boy with the fierce eyes and what his test results predicted lay ahead of him. She phoned his mother, allaying her fears as best she could, telling her they'd be there shortly.

Emotionally drained by her own concerns, she wondered just what use she'd be, but she washed her face and arms in the washroom, brushed her hair, then put on fresh makeup. It was the least she could do for the little boy and his family.

Alex saw her walk out, her head held high, her hair gleaming. He thought about the way she'd kissed him only that morning, and knew she didn't—couldn't—mean the 'no' she'd kept saying, although she'd seemed to think she did.

But, whatever she thought, he had to get her to change her mind, because they were meant to be together and he was damned if he was going to let her forget it.

Unconsciously he'd followed her out the staff exit, and now saw the man she was meeting—with her shiny hair and confident tilt to her head.

Well, Josh Phillips could go to hell as well!

CHAPTER NINE

GABI tied Kirsten's scarf around her head, thinking about Alex and Kirsten. Maybe she should be concentrating on getting Kirsten a man rather than finding one for herself.

Her gaze slid sideways to Josh. What was it about him that had ruined all other men for her friend? And what did Josh have hidden in his past that made him shy away from commitment?

'You're looking very serious,' Josh said, when they pulled up at a set of lights.

'I was thinking about relationships,' she said, and he reached over to give her a sympathetic pat on the shoulder.

'Alex coming back thrown you into a spin, has it?'

'Literally!' Gabi agreed. 'I no longer know which way is up.'

'Then get back together with him. Word around the hospital always was that the Grahams' match was definitely one for the long haul. Although you were both little more than kids when you got married, people figured you had the staying power.'

'Well, people figured wrong,' Gabi reminded him. 'We're divorced—at least I think we are. I signed some papers but I don't know whether it's a two-stage thing.'

'You can always get married again,' Josh said, when she'd directed him to turn off the main ring road onto a feeder road into the McKennas' suburb.

Gabi didn't answer, pretending to be engrossed in the map and the streets through which they were passing, but Josh wasn't easily put off.

'Couldn't you?' he persisted.

'No! As it happens, we couldn't. Well, not right now and maybe never, and I don't want to talk about it—and I don't know where someone like you gets off, Josh Phillips, telling me I should get married again when even thinking of a long-term relationship brings you out in hives.'

She was so furious she spat the words at him, but was he put out? Not one bit. In fact, he laughed at her rage, and then agreed with her assessment.

'Yes, it does, doesn't it?' he said, still chuckling. 'But I'm not you—or Alex. You two were different. Special.'

I don't want to think about it, she wanted to yell, but doubted whether it would do much good. She might shut Josh up but she couldn't turn off her thoughts. Like a wheel turning endlessly in her head, she always came back to it—to the past and the loss of hope for the future.

'Next street on the left,' she said, as they drove down an avenue lined with blooming jacaranda trees, the faint but all-pervading scent of the purple blossoms easing a little comfort into her over-burdened soul.

Then Josh pulled up outside the house, and all personal concerns were forgotten. Right now, the job in hand was to convince these people that leukaemia was treatable and most childhood leukaemia was now curable.

Mr and Mrs McKenna were waiting at the front door, obviously concerned that a doctor from the hospital wanted to visit them. Gabi left the talking to Josh, and was impressed by his honesty and his air of such assurance that she found herself trusting him as much as the couple obviously did.

'We'd like you to bring Michael to the hospital tomorrow. He'll be anaesthetised and we'll do a bone-marrow test—it's not an operation, but it hurts, and it looks fearsome as we put a needle through into the hip bone to with-

draw marrow. We'll also do some scans and X-rays so w
have a good overall view of his whole body.'

He paused, waiting for his listeners to catch up, perhaj
ask questions, then as the silence grew, he continued.

'I know most of this doesn't sink in all at once, so the
are plenty of people in the kids' oncology section who ca
explain things to you bit by bit. And there are always oth
parents there as well, so talk to them. If leukaemia is co
firmed, we'll start treatment immediately. He'll be in ho
pital for four to eight weeks for that first intensive treatme
and one of you can always stay with him if you want to.

The couple, hands clasped together, looked at each oth
and nodded, and Gabi felt tears mist her eyes as she imag
ined the horror in their hearts and minds.

'My mother's here now, minding the kids out in the pla
room, so we could listen in peace. We knew it must be ba
for you to bother coming. She'll come whenever she
needed so we can be with him.'

Josh went on to talk about the treatment, telling them
the new drug which had been used with tremendous succe
and fewer side-effects in the United States, and was no
on trial here.

'It will depend on the bone-marrow tests, of course, b
if it's the type of cancer we think it is, this drug should b
the most effective.'

'You don't have to say yes or no to anything just yet
Gabi put in. 'You need to talk about it, and explain
Michael that he's going to hospital. That's probably enoug
for you to handle tonight. As Josh said, once you're in th
ward there are plenty of people who will answer question
or sit and talk things through with you.'

Mr and Mrs McKenna nodded in unison, and Gabi coul
imagine the numbness of shock both would be feeling.

'Do you want to ask anything now?' Josh said, and thi

me they both shook their heads, but Gabi remained seated, nowing the questions would come as soon as the shock ore off. Mrs McKenna's were practical—would Michael eed slippers, a dressing-gown? Would the other children e allowed to visit? Then Mr McKenna asked about side-ffects of the drug, and what would happen if it didn't ork.

'I hate that part of the job,' Josh said, when they were riving away much later.

'You don't have to do it, do you?' Gabi asked him, still urprised by this ultra-compassionate side of Josh.

'If they're referred on by a GP they know and trust, I an get him or her to do it, but if not I prefer to see the arents myself,' he said. 'Particularly with the drug trials e're conducting. I think it's only fair the families know s much as they can handle. So someone who can answer ne questions is the best person to tell them. I know that at nat first meeting shock blocks most of what I tell them, ut at least if they feel they know me well enough to ask uestions later, I feel I've done my job.'

Ultra-, ultra-compassionate! So why so uncommitted?

Thinking about Josh took her mind off her own prob-ems, and when he suggested she join him for a quick din-er at Mickey's when he dropped her home, she thought f Alex having fun at Kirsten's and agreed.

'Though I'll leave you to order. Tell Mickey I'll have is special penne. I have to dash upstairs for ten minutes. m pet-sitting at the moment, and Alana's lot will be ri-ting if I'm any later than this.'

She fed the animals, brushed the tangles the scarf hadn't revented out of her hair, then walked back down the stairs the foyer to make up for the walk she'd missed on the ay home. Opting for no more diets was one thing, but iving up exercise wasn't an option.

'They're over by the window,' Mickey said to her whe
she walked in.

'They are?' Gabi queried, and Mickey looked puzzle
but as she rounded the bar she saw what he'd mean
Kirsten, Alex and Josh were all seated at a table that looke
out over the pool. Had Josh chosen to sit with them becaus
he wanted to see Kirsten, or because he was match-makin
between Alex and herself?

Whatever the reason, Alex was obviously unhappy wit
the situation. He was scowling at Josh as if the man wer
a mortal enemy and the look he cast at Gabi wasn't exactl
welcoming.

At least Kirsten looked pleased to see her!

Alex watched Gabi trip across the room as if eating wit
her ex-husband and her latest admirer—he refused to con
sider Josh might be more than that—was an everyday oc
currence. He wanted to growl, and possibly punch some
one—preferably Josh—and regretted that his upbringin
prevented him from giving in to the urge. He was sure
would have released some of the tension simmering in hi
body.

As the others chatted he studied Gabi, trying to work ou
if she was feeling a similar amount of stress.

Not noticeably. In fact, she was talking and listening an
smiling with unnecessary animation—showing off for Jos
no doubt—while all Alex could think of was that morning'
kiss and her passionate response—cut short by the 'nc
she'd kept repeating.

A sudden cessation of conversation made him loo
around, to find all three of his companions smiling expec
tantly at him.

Damn! Someone must have asked him a question. Ha
it been about Edinburgh?

Or maybe his mother's progress?

'I think he goes back into the specialty programme next year,' Gabi said, 'though whether they'll take him if he's still comatose I don't know.'

The others laughed and Alex added teasing to the score he had to settle with his ex-wife. Though that morning hadn't been a tease—Gabi's reaction had been genuine, which made the 'no' even more confusing.

Josh was talking about the restructuring of the children's ICU and isolation rooms.

'Of course, we've had to upgrade the isolation rooms since meningococcal raised its ugly head.'

'Have you had a bad season of it?' Alex asked, pleased to have something other than Gabi to focus on, and knowing the disease was always worse in winter.

'Bad enough,' Josh told him. 'We vaccinate all children who come in contact with anyone who develops it, but we're looking into mass vaccinations of the two- to five-year-olds.'

'But what about the other group in danger—the late teens and early twenties?' Kirsten asked.

'At the moment we can't do them all. I think now hospital staff and GPs are more aware of the signs and symptoms we should be able to treat it more quickly and effectively, though once it takes hold there's little that can be done.'

The conversation turned the talk to other 'new' diseases, which, although they'd always existed, were now becoming less rare.

'Someone's buzzing,' Kirsten said, and all of them patted at clothes as if expecting to find a pager in a pocket.

Josh withdrew his and looked at the little screen.

'It's not me,' he said.

'Mine's upstairs so it's not me either,' Alex remarked,

then his chest tightened as he watched Gabi scrabble around in her handbag, finally pulling out the small black receiver.

'Me!' she said. 'Now, if I can find my phone in here—why didn't you tell me to buy smaller handbags, Kirsten?—I'll find out who wants me.'

Alex relaxed. If it was the hospital she'd have recognised the number. But anxiety lingered as she stood up and walked away from them to make her call, and grew to near panic when he saw her face pale.

She walked back to the table.

'I'm sorry, I have to go. A burst water main in one of those new developments up on the hills on the edge of town has caused a landslide. Several apartment blocks have come down. I've been called up for the rescue helicopter.'

The smile that wobbled on her lips broke Alex's composure.

'You can't go. You're not properly trained.' He was on his feet and moving towards the door. 'I'll go. I'll take your car.'

Gabi caught his arm and stopped his progress.

'Go up and check your pager. You've probably been called to the hospital or the site. You can't muck up the emergency response rosters.'

She glanced back at Josh.

'Keep your pager handy, too,' she said, then she slipped past Alex, who was still considering her words about emergency response. She was right. When disaster struck it was imperative everyone obeyed orders or there'd be further chaos. Maybe Gabi would remain in the chopper, treating patients as they were ferried to hospital.

Gabi raced down to her car and drove swiftly to the rescue service base. The helicopter was on the pad outside its shed, the motor running but the rotors not yet moving.

'Good girl!' She was so pleased to see it was Pete piloting the machine she didn't object to the 'girl'. 'That's Chad's motorbike coming in now. He'll be handling things up here for you. It's a simple operation. Apparently some people on the upper floors of some of the units have managed to get to the roof—with their mobiles. The whole structure's so unstable we don't want to put more pressure on it by putting more than one person down there—and a lightweight at that. You'll stay harnessed, and can check them out, then we can lift them off in order of the severity of their injuries.'

He was strapping her into her harness as he explained, reminding her of the equipment attached to it, especially the two-way radio which would keep her in contact with the helicopter.

Chad arrived and Pete climbed into his seat, leaving Chad to ensure Gabi was buckled into hers. Then the rotors roared and the small aircraft lifted, Chad indicating to Gabi to put on the headphones hooked over the back of her seat.

Once airborne, they could easily pick out their destination on the other side of the city, as arc lights mounted on cranes already lit the scene. Coming closer, the buildings looked like a child's model that had been carelessly kicked so it lay tilted and in pieces on the ground.

'I'll come in over the lights and you'll see where we're heading. We'll hook a second line and double harness onto you, Gabi, so we can be lifting people off while you're working. Ask for any equipment you need.'

Pete was so matter-of-fact Gabi had no time to feel anything but the rush of adrenalin any emergency provoked, though when they were hovering over the buildings, and Chad attached her harness to the winch line, a tremor of fear rattled her bones and stiffened her sinews.

Not now, she told it as Chad went over her instructions again. He was watching her with concern and she knew he'd have preferred to be going in her place, as Alex would have, but she was small and light and less likely to cause any further problem to the building's balance.

Then the helicopter dropped until the people beneath it could almost touch it. Gabi slid forward and, as Pete had suggested she'd be doing, she jumped out of the machine, the harness taking her weight, Chad above her, judging to perfection when to stop the winch.

A babble of voices crowded her ears, though the noise of the helicopter was making it difficult to hear.

'My husband,' a woman said. 'He's bleeding badly. He got me up here, then collapsed. And I think Mrs Cochrane's had a heart attack.'

Great! Gabi thought, but she'd seen enough, and she unhitched the second line and used the double harness to hook up a woman and young baby.

'There are two people who need urgent help,' she told Pete through the two-way, while strapping in the woman and trying to calm the others. 'I'll need stretchers for both of them, so I'm unhooking my line harness and I'll send someone else up in it with a woman and baby in the other one. She's ready now, Chad.'

'You're supposed to stay hitched up,' Pete told her.

'As far as weight's concerned, I'm only taking the place of the people you're lifting off,' she reminded him. 'You'll need to take these first people to safety, so I'll stay here and stabilise the injured ones. Just drop the stretchers before you go.'

Pete stopped arguing, and the first group of survivors was winched back into the helicopter, then the lines were lowered again, with the stretchers and the emergency equipment which was kept strapped to them.

Mrs Cochrane was breathing and her pulse seemed strong enough, so Gabi found the man with the bleeding head. He was unconscious but there was nothing she could do about that here. She bound his head and with help from his wife and another man rolled him onto the stretcher. She could hear the helicopter returning and she decided she'd have it lift this patient first, then return for the second one.

She knelt beside Mrs Cochrane, all movement hampered by the tilted floor beneath their feet. The woman was deeply unconscious, though her pupils showed a response to the light Gabi shone in her eyes. With help from the same people, Gabi rolled the woman onto the second stretcher. When the helicopter returned, she waited for the wire rope to be lowered and caught it, attaching it to the stretcher with the head-injured man, checking all the cables were properly secured and not twisted.

'You can lift him now,' she said to Chad, but she stayed where she was, steadying the stretcher until it was out of reach.

'Now you,' she told the injured man's wife, and she strapped her into the second harness. 'Up you go.'

'That just leaves four of us,' the man who'd been helping said. 'Mrs Cochrane will go next, I'm guessing.'

Gabi nodded. 'And one of you,' she told him, nodding towards another younger man who was over by the edge, looking down at the people working to get victims out of the rubble beneath them.

'He can go,' her helper said. 'He's younger and got more to live for. Besides, it's a long time since I've been on a rooftop with a pretty girl.'

The chopper returned and once again Gabi hooked a stretcher to the first cable, then, as it rose, she crossed the roof to tell the young man he was next. The light from the chopper hit his face and she recognised him. Robin Blair! Was that his name?

She called to him, felt something give, then heard a roar and blackness enveloped her.

Gabi looked up into Alex's eyes, so dark with pain they looked almost black, and smiled.

'I felt the earth move,' she whispered hoarsely. 'Was it like that for you?'

He watched consciousness fade from her eyes almost before they closed, and gripped her hand more tightly. He knew he should be talking to her, trying to pierce the coma enveloping her, but he was too tired, and too grateful she was alive, and too wrung out emotionally to do anything but sit there and will her to get better.

'Any change?'

He turned to see his mother, with Fred behind her, wheeling her in a wheelchair.

Alex shook his head, then realised there had been a change.

'She woke up and spoke, but apparently she did that in the ambulance as well.' She'd said 'Where's Alex?' according to reports, and that had kept his hope alive.

'Let me sit with her for a while,' his mother said. 'You need some rest and I'm not going anywhere. Her parents will be here tomorrow, but until they arrive you'll have to bear the brunt of it, so rest now while you have the chance.'

It made sense—when didn't his mother make sense?—but he didn't want to leave Gabi, even for a minute.

'Come on, Alex,' Fred said quietly. 'I'll take you home and wait there so I can drive you back as soon as you've had a sleep. Your mother won't rest until you do. You know that.'

Alex looked at the man he'd resented for so long, and nodded to acknowledge the truth of his words. Then he kissed Gabi, kissed his mother and left, not resenting at all the hand Fred rested on his shoulder.

Gabi lay in her nether world for six days. Her parents alternated at her bedside, with Alex there most of the time as well, leaving only to eat and sleep, apologising to the hospital but knowing they could get an agency doctor to take his place in A and E. After all, he'd only been a fill-in himself.

So he was with her when she finally, and fully, awoke.

'I'm in hospital? Our hospital?'

She took in her surroundings with the lost expression he'd seen on so many recovering patients, then alarm flickered in her eyes and she started up in the bed, looking around frantically, holding up her hands as if to inspect them.

'Hell! Am I bleeding? Did I bleed? Did everyone know I'm suspect?'

The words made no sense at all to Alex, who tried to calm her, but as her cries became increasingly hysterical, and it seemed to be his presence that was upsetting her more than anything, he left the room to find Catherine Cross, the doctor who was in charge of her case.

'Keep Alex away,' he heard Gabi say as Catherine walked into the room.

The words scored through his skin and he felt a coldness as if they'd cut his heart and blood was leaking out. She'd wanted him when she was semi-conscious, but now her senses had returned she'd rejected him again.

'She doesn't know what she's saying,' Gabi's mother told him. She'd been in the room and, perhaps realising he'd heard Gabi's rejection, had come out to be with him.

To comfort him?

There *was* no comfort. He'd been at the triage area over

a hundred metres from the building when the second collapse had occurred and, on hearing Gabi had been trapped, had joined the men digging by hand, desperate to reach survivors before air pockets ran out. Though his desperation had all been for the woman he loved.

Loved dearly and for ever. And now it *couldn't* be too late for them to sort things out. Fate couldn't be so cruel. Not to Gabi, who deserved at least to know how he felt about her, and to hear him apologise for all the pain he'd caused her in the past.

So he'd dug, and they'd found children, and other adults, but he hadn't been the one to find her. Someone else had, when the long night and another day had ended, and they had been finding fewer and fewer people alive.

'Why was she so worried about blood?'

Nancy Kerr's question jolted him and he turned to look at Gabi's mother who was suffering nearly as much as he was.

'What did you say?'

'I wondered why Gabi was so upset about blood and bleeding. It's not as if she's ever minded it. Out on the farm she was always the one to patch up wounded animals. She had a cat she stitched up with embroidery thread when she was only six.'

Alex had heard the story before, but he nodded acknowledgement of the retelling of the tale while his mind whirled back to Gabi's first coherent words—if you didn't count asking for him and questioning the moving of the earth.

'Did I bleed?' she'd said. Then what? He frowned as he tried to recall the fragment of memory.

Something about being suspect.

And something had happened to change her direction in life—Alana had suggested perhaps someone young had died. But what if it hadn't been that? What if it had been that common but dreaded occurrence, a needle-stick injury?

She'd kissed him, then panicked when things might have gone further. She'd be covered for hep. B—all hospital personnel had regular shots—but did she fear HIV?

He kissed his ex-mother-in-law, pushed her back towards Gabi's room and said, 'You stay with her. I'll be right back.'

He headed for the lift and down to A and E. He wouldn't be able to access results of her blood tests—it was near impossible to access your own—but if she'd had a needle-stick injury in A and E there'd be an incident report. Could he access them?

Though even if the donor was positive for HIV Gabi wouldn't know if she was—not yet! But the injury could have happened six months ago and she'd now tested positive.

His heart faltered, then he realised that if that had been the case there'd have been a notation on her file—a warning for all staff to be double-gloved—and he'd read her file every day. Which meant it had to be a recent injury and as yet unconfirmed.

He sighed as the lift spilled him out on the ground floor. He'd been forgetting her over-developed sense of responsibility. However slight the chances—and the figures were so slight they barely counted—Gabi wouldn't want to risk passing the infection on to anyone, let alone someone she loved.

Or *had* loved?

No, he refused to believe their love was dead. She wouldn't have kissed him the way she had the morning he'd gone down to talk to her. Wouldn't have looked at him, when she'd woken briefly the day before, with so much love in her eyes he'd felt his bones melt.

Roz was at the desk.

'How is she?'

'Awake, but there's something bothering her. I think it goes back to her last week on night duty. Do you keep the incident reports going back that far or have they gone into central filing?'

Roz crossed to the filing cabinet.

'You're not supposed to have access to other people's incident reports,' she told him, but she'd pulled out a drawer and was riffling through it. 'But I could talk to myself as I read it. Last night on night duty. Needle-stick injury, donor refused to have blood tested. Name here, and an address in Sydney, so it's a bit difficult to check him out, but a refusal to be tested usually signifies the donor either knows he's positive for something or suspects he might be but doesn't want to know.'

'But wouldn't Gabi have had HIV prophylaxis just in case?' he demanded.

Roz raised her eyebrows.

'Come on, Alex, you know how many needle-stick injuries there are in A and E each year—hundreds, if not thousands. If the patient's a known case of either HIV or AIDS, then, yes, we treat immediately—but for every needle-stick injury? That's why we try to always get donor blood. And most times we do—sometimes we don't.'

'But Gabi won't know until she's been tested at what—three and six months?'

'I think that's right, but think about it. Even if you suspected you might have contracted it, how would you feel?'

'Numb?' Alex suggested.

Or determined to get the most out of life, to try new things, get a new image, live life to the full? What had Gabi said to him that day he'd arrived? Something about dancing all night?

Well, Gabi Graham, he said to himself as he walked away from the desk, that's just what we'll do. That and more. Kirsten had mentioned dancing lessons—he could do that! He might whinge a bit, but he could do it.

And together they'd face whatever fears and demons she was nursing inside her. Together they'd conquer them—or, if the million-to-one shot came off, at least they'd put up a good fight. Hell! Hundreds of people lived for years and years without HIV becoming full-blown AIDS. Boy, did that woman need a talking-to!

He stormed back upstairs and was confronted by an empty room.

'They've shifted her to Bayview Private,' the nurse on duty at the desk told him. 'Her parents felt if she stayed here, now she's conscious, there'd be a constant stream of hospital staff popping in to see her, and what she needs more than anything is rest. Dr Cross agreed.'

I guess they had the right, Alex conceded grimly as he went back down in the lift, but the realisation stung. Gabi had been his—not a possession but a partner—for so long, it was hard to feel he could no longer make decisions on her behalf.

Though there was one decision he would make for her— the one about her determination to keep him at arm's length.

He was walking out of the hospital when it struck him that not only did he not have the means of getting to Bayview Private, but he had no idea where Gabi's car was even if he had the right to use it.

Damn and blast. He should have thought of that earlier. He'd organised for her parents to stay in the flat and he had shifted to Alana's to feed the animals, but Gabi's car must still be at the rescue service base. Would the keys also be there?

He hesitated, then hailed a cab. She'd be undergoing admittance procedures at Bayview, so he'd go out and get her car first, then ask her if he could use it while she was in hospital.

It was a sensible idea, but for some reason it bred uncertainty within him. Perhaps because he was assuming in all these plans that Gabi would agree, when in actual fact he couldn't be entirely certain of anything the new Gabi was likely to do.

Or what anyone else would do, he discovered when he arrived at the rescue base to find her car had been collected by Kirsten days earlier. Of course, by the time he'd talked to Pete in an effort to discover what had happened to it, and discussed the rescue effort, the taxi had long gone and he had to wait until Pete finished some maintenance work, then catch a lift with him.

'I went to see the chap they pulled out with Gabi,' Pete told him. 'Have you seen him? He's in your hospital. Two broken legs but otherwise OK, or as OK as anyone will ever be after being buried alive for a couple of days. Apparently he knew Gabi.'

Alex was kind of listening, but at the same time he was wondering if he could ask Pete to go out of his way and drop him at Bayview, so when Pete said that the man wanted Gabi to visit him, and would Alex ask her if she'd do it when she was feeling better, he had to ask Pete to start again.

'A chap called Robert Blaine. He was on the top of the building with Gabi when it collapsed. We'd just winched up an older woman who was comatose—turned out she'd taken her sleeping tablets and simply passed out. Another man still on the roof was killed, but Robert and Gabi ended up under the slab of concrete that somehow folded over them instead of crushing them.'

Alex shivered, though the day was hot and Pete had the windows open rather than running the air-conditioning.

'I'll ask her,' he promised Pete, 'though it's not as easy now she's been shifted.' He explained how Gabi had been transferred and was pleased when Pete offered to drop him at Bayview—saved him having to ask.

But getting to Bayview was one thing—seeing Gabi was another.

'She's sleeping,' Nancy told him, meeting him outside the door after a nurse had asked him to wait. The older woman was looking so distressed that Alex guessed what it was she didn't want to say.

'She doesn't want to see me?' he said bleakly, and Nancy, tears brimming from her eyes, took his hand and squeezed it tightly.

'I'm sure she doesn't know what she's saying,' she said, accepting Alex's hug and wiping tears from her eyes. 'But while she's still so unstable it might be better...'

Alex kissed her cheek.

'I know—there's no point in fighting with her now.' Then he grinned at Nancy. 'But be sure of one thing, ex-mother-in-law of mine, I do intend to fight. Not only to fight, but to win.'

The battle commenced the day Gabi arrived home. Alex might have established himself in Alana's flat, and had even bought a new spare bed so he wasn't fighting the bed spring now Alana had returned, but he had filled Gabi's flat with flowers and balloons—red heart-shaped balloons announcing his love. And if her parents were embarrassed by it, too bad, he'd decided. In fact, embarrassment might be good, because the sooner they went back to the farm and left him to look after her, the better.

He also sent her letters, and tempting treats, but didn't

mention that he knew about the needle-stick—she was still recuperating and he didn't want her suffering a setback. Besides, being Gabi, her instincts would be to protect him, and he'd have to break down all the barriers she put up, slowly and patiently—one by one.

Three days after she came out of hospital, as her parents prepared to leave, he made his move, coming up to the flat on the pretext of helping them carry their bags down to the car, but doing no more than nodding at Gabi to acknowledge her presence.

He could see his behaviour threw her, and guessed she wanted to talk to him—if only to tell him to stop sending her flowers—but he didn't linger, merely mentioning he was available if she wanted any shopping done, and he'd be calling each day to see that she was OK.

'I don't need you coming. Kirsten will check on me—in fact, everyone's fussing so much the attention's likely to cause a setback.'

'Kirsten's an occupational therapist, not a doctor, and I won't fuss,' he told her, and departed before she had a chance to get a bit more off her chest.

'You will look after her?' Nancy asked as he lifted her suitcase into the car boot.

'Of course he will,' Ross Kerr answered for him, then he turned and shook Alex's hand. 'And you'll sort out whatever nonsense there is between you and Gabi, won't you, son?'

The anxiety in the man's voice tightened Alex's throat.

'I'll do my darnedest,' he promised, though as they drove away he realised he was far less certain than he'd sounded. His Gabi had a lot of sterling characteristics, but she could be as stubborn as a mule once she'd made up her mind—especially when the welfare of a loved one was at stake.

And if his guess was correct, and she'd decided that not

seeing him was the only way to protect him, then changing her mind about that wasn't going to be easy. What he had to do was prove his love to her in such a way it would sweep her off her feet and into his arms.

For ever.

CHAPTER TEN

NOT that it would be easy, Alex admitted to himself. Fo
a start, talk wouldn't work. He could talk himself blue i
the face and not get Gabi to agree. No, this was the tim
for action.

But what action?

He went back to work, but on night duty so he'd b
available during the day, when fewer people were in th
apartments.

He e-mailed her daily, not pressuring her exactly, bu
sending jokes he'd heard or received, scanned photos he'
taken in Scotland, with the odd one from their marriag
thrown in. He sent her parcels of enticing food, left book
and magazines outside her door and generally made it im
possible for her to forget about him.

'Join the Latin-American dancing lessons,' Kirsten sug
gested. 'She's going to those next week.'

Alex considered it, then realised that if Gabi turned u
and saw him there she'd be likely to walk away and she'
miss something to which she'd been looking forward. Bu
dancing...something she knew he hated... How would tha
fit the action scenario?

Worth a try!

He phoned the school and arranged to attend th
Saturday morning classes—he'd learn to dance if it kille
him.

Gabi went along to her first dancing class because she knew
she had to get out of the flat and she was damned if she

vas going to let one little life-threatening accident knock
ut all her newly acquired backbone. It would also get her
ut of the flat, where memories of Alex were becoming so
ll-pervading they were consuming her.

Kirsten and Alana had both pointed out he'd proved his
ove for her by now, and she could hardly tell them it
vasn't a matter of him proving his love so much as keeping
im safe. That secret she hugged to herself. In another few
nonths she'd know, one way or another, and until then...

She danced—and enjoyed it. And went back to work,
nd enjoyed that as well, especially as the transfer to the
aediatric ward had come through and there was little
hance of running into Alex.

Then the flowers, e-mails and little gifts slowed to a
rickle, and eventually stopped, and a void as big as the
ne she'd suffered when Alex had left her opened up in
er life. She started doing things she'd said she wouldn't
o—going out with Alana and Kirsten to parties she found
reary and uninteresting.

'So how's Alex?' Ever so casually, she asked Alana one
ate afternoon when they'd both come off duty at the same
me so were walking home together.

'He seems fine—though I don't see much of him because
e's working nights. I don't know where he disappears to
t weekends.'

Alana cast a sidelong glance at Gabi. It had been Daisy's
dvice to Alex that he stop sending the flowers and gifts,
er theory being that now Gabi was used to them a sudden
essation might make her think differently about things. Jolt
er a little.

And as far as Alana could tell it had worked.

'Don't tell me that now you've finally got the message
cross that you don't want his notes and gifts and flowers,
ou're actually missing them.'

'Of course I'm not!' Gabi said crossly, thinking that self sacrifice was really the pits.

But she *was* missing them, and him, and her heart ache with the hopelessness of it all. The hospital hierarchy ha suggested she take some time off, and she was tempted t do just that. She could go home, back to the farm, and sta there until she knew for certain.

By which time Alex would probably have met and mar ried someone else!

And it would mean missing her dance lessons, whic were the one bright spot in her life just now, and the end of-term Christmas dance in a fortnight, which all her fellov enthusiasts assured her was the best night of the year.

Yeah?

So she stayed, and worked, and danced, thinking of he dreams—her list—and all she'd wanted to accomplish Actually, she'd done well by the list, really succeeded witl everything on it—except the dancing-all-night part, and tha had been a bit silly anyway.

In that case, shouldn't she be feeling confident and pos itive, instead of hurting and depressed?

Thinking of the list reminded her of Pete and the rescu service. She should go out and see them. She knew she wa off the roster, but now that the doctors had pronounced he fit surely she could go back on it.

'Did you ever catch up with that chap they rescued jus before you?' Pete asked, when the politenesses were out o the way.

'What chap?'

Pete frowned.

'I thought I told you—or maybe I told Alex and he wa going to pass the message on. There was a youngish mar on the roof with you, and you were both trapped under th

ame slab. I visited him in hospital and he particularly
asked to see you.'

But, much as Gabi tried to remember, the actual accident
remained locked in some unreachable part of her memory.

'The last thing I remember is going down onto the roof—
everything else I know is what people have told me.'

'That happens,' Pete agreed, 'but the fellow was really
keen to make contact. In fact, it was upsetting him so much
I promised I'd see to it. Can you find out from the hospital
lists who he was? He was on the fourth floor in the hospital,
two broken legs.'

Two days later Gabi found herself unexpectedly free to
take a proper lunch-hour, but with Jane out of hospital and
Alana off duty she was debating whether to go to the canteen or slip home for a while when Pete's words came back
to her.

The person she'd been buried with had been on the
fourth floor. Even with two broken legs, unless complications had set in, he'd be long gone by now, but maybe she
could track him down. He might remember more than she
did, and according to the therapist the hospital had insisted
she see talking about the accident was good for her.

'Robert Blaine. I've got a contact phone number for him,
care of his parents, because of course his home was one
which was lost in the landslide. I can't give you his number,
but if you like I can give him a call and ask if he still wants
to see you. I know he asked for you quite often, so I guess
he would.'

The nurse phoned the number and Robert answered. On
being told Gabi was enquiring, he insisted on speaking to
her.

'I'm kind of tied up right now,' he joked, 'but I really
would like to see you. Would you mind coming here?'

Had he sensed hesitation? Because he added, 'I'm well

chaperoned by Mum, so even if you can't run faster tha
a man with two pinned legs you'll be quite safe.'

'I wasn't worried about that,' Gabi assured him. 'If
hesitated, it was because your voice seemed familiar. Do
know you?'

'Come and see for yourself,' he said, and again Gab
found his voice prodding at memory cells in her brai
Though voices were often distorted by the phone so it coul
be an illusion.

She made arrangements to call the following Saturda
morning, wrote down his address and instructions on th
easiest way to get to his part of the city and hung up.

But after a late day on Friday, and an even later nigh
with Kirsten and Alana in Mickey's bar, by Saturday morn
ing visiting a fellow survivor was the last thing she felt lik
doing.

Still, she crawled out of bed, showered and dressed, the
took the lift down to the basement. As she passed the sec
ond floor she wondered where Alex was and what he wa
doing. Did the fact that he'd stopped pestering her mea
he'd finally taken her no for no and backed away—which
she both did and didn't want him to do—or that he'd foun
someone else?

That thought killed whatever smidgen of pleasure the da
might have held, so in a mood of deepening gloom sh
drove across town.

'Robert Blaine?' she asked, peering at the man wh
opened the door to her, checking he did indeed have ex
ternal scaffolding on both broken legs. 'But...'

She knew him—just couldn't place him—but she wa
fairly certain it wasn't from the accident.

'Come in,' he said, taking her hand and leading her int
a pleasant, sunny sitting room. 'This is my mother, Ruth

ho's provided this great spread and will now leave us to
lk. I asked her to stay so you'd know she existed.'

Gabi introduced herself to the woman, then sat down,
ccepting coffee and a freshly made muffin. Mrs Blaine,
atisfied Gabi had been looked after, retreated, and Robert
egan.

'You don't remember me, do you?' he said, with a smile
hat would have charmed birds out of trees.

'I know I know you, but if I saw you on the roof I
uppose it's from there.'

Robert hesitated.

'You recognised me on the roof. My last memory before
verything went black was of you coming towards me.'

This time the hesitation was longer.

'You called me Robin Blair.'

Gabi closed her eyes and the world swirled around her.
he'd survived an accident that had killed so many other
eople—now he was going to tell her it was only tempo-
ary.

'Are you OK? I'm sorry to do it this way. I was going
o come to the hospital and tell you in person—show you
he papers—but then there was the accident, and of course
he papers were destroyed, but I've been retested and I'm
lear.'

'You're clear?'

Robert frowned at her.

'Are you sure you're OK?'

Gabi managed a nod.

'Do you remember where we met? At the hospital early
ne Saturday morning. You jabbed yourself with a needle
nd I wouldn't let you test my blood.'

Gabi nodded again. Then, in case that wasn't definite
nough, said, 'I remember all that, but what are you tel-
ing me?'

He tried the smile, but this time it was more shamefaced than anything.

'I'm gay—always have been—and for the last four years I've been in a relationship. Bill, my partner—I love him, I really do—but about eight months ago things started going...not wrong, but kind of stale. I know this sounds as if I'm making excuses, and I am. I should have made more of an effort to fix things because I knew it was only me who was unhappy. Bill was just motoring along.'

Like herself and Alex, Gabi thought, then terrible fear filled her and she had to break in.

'Bill, your partner—was he in the flat? Was he harmed?'

She was imagining how she'd have felt if it had been Alex, and the mere thought was enough to accelerate her heartbeats.

This time Robin's smile was more heartfelt.

'No. He's an engineer and had been away—in fact, he's still away, though he did fly home for a week while I was in hospital. His contract's nearly finished and he's due back next week. I guess I'm using the fact that things weren't good between us before he went away as an excuse, but I met this other fellow and it wasn't until we'd had a bit of a fling that he told me he was HIV positive.'

'You weren't using protection?' Gabi gasped. 'That's just plain stupid.'

'We did most of the time,' Robert told her, 'just once or twice without, and then I realised it was nothing more than me getting back at Bill. I'd really been upset about him accepting the overseas contract when he knew I couldn't go, and the whole thing was just a disaster.'

'So?' Gabi demanded. 'If you were feeling all this guilt why not tell me you might be HIV positive?'

'I didn't want to worry you—well, that's my excuse. But in truth I panicked, thought I could be sued or get into

ouble for doing it to you, and then I excused myself by
lling myself I'd been negative at the three-month test so
ou should be OK.'

'You could have told me that as well,' Gabi fumed. Then
he realised none of this was the point. 'And now?' she
sked.

The smile came back, but genuine this time.

'I'm clean,' he said. 'I received the results of the last test
he day of the accident—that's why I was on the roof.
tupid, really—I was yelling my delight at the sky! And,
lease believe me, Dr Graham, I was going to track you
own the very next day and explain. Then I saw you com-
ng towards me across the roof...'

'The caving-in thing must have seemed like divine ret-
ibution,' she remarked, not totally satisfied with all of this.
Why did you give a false name and address at the hospital
he morning you were brought in?'

At least he looked embarrassed!

'I'd been going to the hospital for testing. I thought if
ny name went into the computer it would show I was on
he "suspicious" list and that might worry you.'

'No more than your equally suspicious behaviour did,'
abi snapped. 'And, for your information, any needle-stick
jury has to be reported and I've been worrying about
ontracting HIV ever since it happened. You've caused me
great deal of anxiety and...'

She stood up—no need to tell this man—who, though
ontrite, would probably do the same thing again to save
is own skin or even embarrassment—that it might also
ave cost her any chance of getting back with Alex.

'I'm sorry. Really, very, very sorry,' Robert bleated as
he marched out the door.

'So you should be!' Gabi snapped, but as she drove home
he realised that a lot of her anger with him was unjustified.

It wasn't his fault that his story about his and Bill's rel
tionship had so many parallels to her relationship wi
Alex.

What had she done to mend the rift between them whe
it had first appeared soon after Alex's father had died a
she'd felt resentment that he hadn't let her share his grie

Not enough, that was for sure.

Then, when he'd announced the Scotland thing, she
yelled and ranted and raved, but had never explained ho
it had made her feel—how upset she'd been that he'd ma
that kind of decision without consulting her.

Then the baby...

But at least now they'd talked about that, though h
heart still ached with remembered pain and more than an
thing she'd have liked to cry out the remnants of her gri
on Alex's shoulder.

Alex?

What was he thinking now?

He'd said he loved her, had shown that love in wor
and deeds since the accident, and though he'd obviousl
been willing to put their past differences behind him a
try again, now she was free to love him, and have him lo
her, he was gone.

Try as she might, she couldn't find out where he disa
peared to when not at work. Sleeping part of the time, f
sure, but subtle questioning of Alana brought no furth
answers. Even blatant questioning of Alana brought not
ing. And throwing a tantrum had only made Alana laugh

'I just want to talk to him—to explain!' Gabi told her.

'He tried hard enough to talk to you from the time h
came back—particularly when you came out of hospita
And you wouldn't listen—wouldn't even see him. Do yo
wonder he doesn't want to talk to you now?'

But it couldn't end like this, could it? Gabi thought

erself. I love him and he loves me—he'd said so in his
otes, and the balloons, and e-mails.

Love like that couldn't just have died so suddenly, could
?

The temptation to retreat into her shell, to curl into a ball
nd hide herself from the world was enormous, but she'd
one that before—when their differences had culminated in
•sing the baby and she'd shut Alex out.

That was the wimp's way.

What had happened to self-focus?

She joined a Thursday dance class as well, to make up
hat she'd missed and because she was determined to once
gain reclaim her life. With only a week to the end-of-term
ance she wanted to perfect all the steps. Maybe there'd be
stranger there and she could dance all night in her sexy
•d dress, then drive to the coast and watch the sun come
ɔ over the ocean.

But the thought lacked the appeal it had had when she'd
dded it to her list so many weeks ago, and she was tempted
• offer her ticket to one of the nurses at work. Helen was
ways complaining about her lack of a social life.

▪ the end she went, dressing in the slinky red dress, think-
▪g all the time of when she'd originally intended to wear
. Though that had been a laugh. Alex, who hated dancing,
ancing all night?

Kirsten drove her to the venue, a nightclub given over
• the dancing school for the evening.

'Because you'll need a drink for sure,' Kirsten said. 'And
ɔu can always get a cab home if no one tall, dark and
andsome offers you a lift. Mind you, the way you look—
•nsational—you might be best off refusing offers. Take
ıeir phone numbers and tell them you'll call, then decide

in the morning who was the cutest. Other numbers you ca[n]
pass on to loveless friends.'

Gabi laughed, but wished she felt more excited. The peo[o]
ple she knew from both her evening classes were pleasan[t]
enough, but a lot of them had gone to the lessons with thei[r]
partners, and the few unattached men she'd met had bee[n]
nice, but that was all.

'Good luck!' Kirsten said, as she pulled up outside th[e]
club.

'I'm not going hunting,' Gabi reminded her. 'I'm onl[y]
going to dance—to put all I've learned into practice.'

'Good luck anyway,' Kirsten repeated, then she smile[d]
waved and drove away.

The smile should have prepared Gabi but, though sh[e]
thought it strange, it didn't mean a thing until she entere[d]
the club, greeted a few people she knew, then made he[r]
way to the bar to get a drink. Natalie, her instructor, cam[e]
towards her with someone—a man, from his height—tai[l]
ing along behind, though in the crush and gloomy light [it]
was hard to tell what he looked like.

'As you're my best student in the Tuesday class, I'v[e]
brought the best from my weekend classes for you to danc[e]
with,' Natalie said, turning and dragging the poor unfo[r]
tunate man into the light of the bar. 'He's been workin[g]
really hard to be ready for tonight.'

Gabi's heart must have recognised Alex a split secon[d]
before her eyes did, for she was sure it had started to ban[g]
against her ribs before she'd properly assimilated his pres[s]
ence.

Assimilating the fact that Alex had taken *dancing* lesson[s]
might take a little longer. Like a century?

But before she could speak—struck dumb didn't begi[n]
to cover it—Alex had taken her hand.

'The music's started. Shall we dance?'

Words wouldn't come, and her body was in such tumult she wasn't certain it would be able to function well enough to move, let alone dance. But Alex's fingers squeezed hers with a reassuring pressure and she followed him onto the floor, then let him take her in his arms and lead her through the intricacies of the lambada.

She felt as if she was floating, high on a cloud of dreams. Her feet moved to the music, her body swayed to the rhythm, and the sense of rightness of just being in Alex's arms was so overwhelming she was beyond speech.

At times they stopped, moving to the bar, where Alex always managed to find a stool for her, then he'd stand behind her, solid and protective, handing her a drink, offering a delicacy from the plates of tapas on the bar. She should be talking—telling him things—explaining—but the feeling of all-pervading rightness was so strong she was afraid words would break the spell.

Then Alex, who from time to time had spoken, but only to suggest they rest or to offer sustenance, brought her up close against his body.

'We need to leave,' he murmured, and when she looked up into his face, intending to ask why, he bent and kissed her. 'Trust me,' he said, and his smile made her heart shiver.

He escorted her down to an underground car park and led the way to a new dark green sedan.

'Did the grapevine tell you I'd bought a new car?' he asked, using a remote control to unlock the doors then handing her into the passenger seat.

'The grapevine's told me nothing,' Gabi said. 'It's been a conspiracy of silence. But if those two, Kirsten and Alana, were in on this, I'll...'

Alex shut the door and walked around the bonnet, climbing in behind the wheel.

'You'll what?' he teased, but oh-so-gently.

Gabi smiled at him.

'I don't know, but they should have said. They know I've been going mad these last few weeks. I thought I'd lost you, Alex. Pushed you so far away I'd never get you back.'

She felt a tremor shoot through her as she spoke—was she assuming too much from a night of dancing? Was he back?

He leant over and kissed her on the lips.

'I found out when I was in Scotland that you could never push me that far, Gabi,' he said, tilting her head so he could look into her eyes. And though the light in the car park was dim, the expression in his eyes told her he spoke the truth. 'Though I didn't realise it at the time and it wasn't until I returned that I understood why I'd come back. Why I had to come back.'

A new tremor, but this time of excitement, skittered through her. They were going home—together—and there was no reason to say no ever again. But when Alex drove out of the car park he turned left towards the suburbs, not right towards the flat.

Disappointment flooded through her. She *had* assumed too much. But where could they be going?

When he took the access to the freeway she stopped guessing and asked.

'Where are we going?'

'Down to the coast. Forty-five minutes to get there, then thirty minutes for the prelude to the sunrise. I checked the time in yesterday's morning's paper.'

'How did you know?' Gabi asked, wondering if she'd left her list of things to do lying around the flat.

Alex turned and grinned at her.

'Remember the first morning I came home? You demanded to know why I'd assumed you'd been at work, not dancing all night in a red dress then watching the sun come up over the ocean.'

She tried to speak, but all that came out were some incoherent splutters.

'I like the red dress, by the way,' he added, then he concentrated on driving, giving Gabi the opportunity to study the man who'd learned to dance so she could fulfil her dream.

And, studying him, she couldn't help noticing a frown furrowing his forehead.

Because he was driving? Surely not. They were on a four-lane highway with barely another vehicle in sight.

Was he still worried she'd push him away?

She was wondering what to say, how to explain, when he glanced her way and then back at the road, as if the words he wanted to use to express himself were better said to the road than directly to her.

'I know about the needle-stick injury. About there being no donor blood and you being under that black cloud of doubt, Gabi, and I know, you being you, you've tried to protect me by pushing me away. But it won't work because without you—sick or well—my life is empty of all joy and wonderment and happiness and everything else that makes living worthwhile.'

He was gripping the steering-wheel so tightly she could see his knuckles gleaming whitely through his skin, and though she knew she should say something—tell him it was all OK—what he was saying had left her breathless and so choked up she'd make a fool of herself if she did more than breathe.

And she'd like to ask him how he knew, given the confidentiality of files in the hospital, but that could wait. Right now Alex was talking again, telling her things her wounded heart had waited so long to hear.

'So, no matter what you say, I'm back, Gabi. Back where I belong, which is by your side and in your bed and forever part of your life. Wherever you are, whatever you do, whatever happens in the future, we'll be together, and we'll share the joys and sorrows—understand me?'

He pulled over into a layby by the emergency phone so he could turn to face her as he made his final point. Then he slid the T-shift into 'Park' and leaned across, taking her shoulders and drawing her close so he could kiss her.

The ever-lightening sky woke Gabi to the fact they might miss the sunrise, and she pulled reluctantly away, then chuckled as Alex cursed and hurriedly put the car back into gear, taking off so hastily the tyres squealed their protest.

'The sunrise isn't all that important,' she told him, but he refused to listen.

'It was part of the plan. We'll make it.'

And make it they did, pulling up in the deserted car park behind the lifesavers' shed when the approaching sun had spread a vivid magenta across the sky but as yet remained hidden itself.

Gabi slipped off her shoes and slid her hand into Alex's, and together they walked across the dunes and down towards the ocean, settling on dry sand above the high-water mark, listening to the waves splashing up on the beach, watching the colours change in the sky and spread out to embrace the world with their vivid beauty.

'I found the donor; he's negative,' Gabi said, as the first fiery tip of the sun appeared on the horizon. 'I know it doesn't matter to you, but it does to me. I couldn't have put you at risk, Alex. Not even the slightest, most minimal risk. I love you far too much for that!'

He pulled her closer to his side, and brushed his lips across her hair.

'Do you think I didn't realise that, you foolish woman?' he murmured, his voice husky with the emotion Gabi could feel in her own heart. 'But I knew I'd have the devil's own job convincing you it didn't matter to me. The cards and flowers and gifts were only the first step; the dancing was the second, to show you how I felt. I must admit I wasn't sure what the third would be if that didn't work, but one thing I *did* know for sure, and that was that I wasn't giving up.'

Silence fell as they watched the sky change colour, then Alex spoke again.

'I handled so many things badly, Gabi, after Dad died. I know you tried to help, but I couldn't talk about it, so I shut you out and tried to lose myself in work. Then, when Mum started seeing Fred just twelve months later, all I could think about was getting away—from them and from all the unresolved stuff I was carting around with me. That's where the idea of studying overseas came from.'

'I should have realised that,' she said quietly, 'but all I felt was hurt that you hadn't consulted me in any of the arrangements.'

She snuggled closer to him.

'You know, Jane said something to me not long after you left. She said she'd come to realise that it was because she'd been so unbelievably happy with your father that she'd wanted to marry again. She said what she felt for Fred was different, just as her love for you was different to her love for your father, but the happiness of being part of a couple was still there.'

Alex sighed, then dropped another kiss on the top of her head.

'I understand that now—in fact, I understand a lot of

things, mainly because I've had time to think about them. You've no idea the amount of time a man has when he no longer has a wife to love and be loved by. There was our estrangement, and losing the baby—all the regrets added up, Gabi, until they were like a weighted cloud, suffocating me. I knew, one way or the other, I had to get out from under it.'

'So you came home?'

'Yes,' he admitted. 'Mum's illness moved the date forward, but I'd booked to come for Christmas anyway. To see Mum, and sort things out with her and Fred, but mainly to see you. To tell you how I felt—how much I loved you.'

Gabi leant against his shoulder, feeling the firm bulk of him, his warmth and, more than anything, his familiarity. He was more than her husband and her lover and her best friend. He was the rock that anchored her to the earth. For the past two years she'd been lost, floating untethered, but now Alex was back.

Something else occurred to her.

'Are we married or divorced?' she asked him.

He grinned at her.

'I'm not sure, but if the divorce has gone through it will give us a chance to do it all again. And, though it might be anticipating things, I've booked the honeymoon suite up there…' he pointed towards the five-star hotel further along the beach '…for the rest of the weekend. Are you ready for breakfast?'

Gabi smiled and snuggled closer.

'Before or after?' she teased, and knew when he pulled her to her feet then held her close that it would probably be after.

Modern Romance™
...seduction and
passion guaranteed

Tender Romance™
...love affairs that
last a lifetime

Sensual Romance™
...sassy, sexy and
seductive

Blaze Romance™
...the temperature's
rising

Medical Romance™
...medical drama on
the pulse

Historical Romance™
...rich, vivid and
passionate

27 new titles every month.

*With all kinds of Romance for
every kind of mood...*

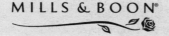

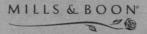

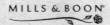

MILLS & BOON

Helen Brooks

Lynne Graham

Kim Lawrence

BUSINESS *Affairs*

Three brand-new stories about falling for the boss

Available from 17th January 2003

*Available at most branches of WH Smith,
Tesco, Martins, Borders, Eason, Sainsbury's
and all good paperback bookshops.*

0203/24/MB62

2 FREE

books and a surprise gift!

We would like to take this opportunity to thank you for reading this Mills & Boon® book by offering you the chance to take TWO more specially selected titles from the Medical Romance™ series absolutely FREE! We're also making this offer to introduce you to the benefits of the Reader Service™—

- ★ FREE home delivery
- ★ FREE gifts and competitions
- ★ FREE monthly Newsletter
- ★ Exclusive Reader Service discount
- ★ Books available before they're in the shops

Accepting these FREE books and gift places you under no obligation to buy, you may cancel at any time, even after receiving your free shipment. Simply complete your details below and return the entire page to the address below. *You don't even need a stamp!*

YES! Please send me 2 free Medical Romance books and a surprise gift. I understand that unless you hear from me, I will receive 4 superb new titles every month for just £2.55 each, postage and packing free. I am under no obligation to purchase any books and may cancel my subscription at any time. The free books and gift will be mine to keep in any case.

M3ZEA

Ms/Mrs/Miss/Mr ....Initials......................................
BLOCK CAPITALS PLEASE
Surname ....
Address ....
....
....Postcode ....

Send this whole page to:
UK: FREEPOST CN81, Croydon, CR9 3WZ
EIRE: PO Box 4546, Kilcock, County Kildare (stamp required)